The Prisoner Of Rubato Towers

Crazed memories of lockdown life in the plague year

By Richard Heller

Cover and Illustrations by Rupert Macnee

Published 2020 by **Xerus Publishing**

204 the School House
Pages Walk
London SE1 4HG
England

Produced and Printed by Print2Demand Limited

1 Newlands Road
Westoning
Bedfordshire MK45 5LD
England

ISBN 978-1-8381654-0-6

All rights reserved. No part of this book may be reproduced or transmitted in any form, electronic or mechanical, including photocopy or any information storage and retrieval system, without permission in writing by the author.

Richard Heller is a man of letters, few of them answered, and a cricketer in the sunset of a career which never really had a dawn. He has been in lockdown at his premises in Rubato Towers, London SE, which he shares with a mouse and two fornicating foxes. He gives regular piano recitals to his neighbours and they bang on the walls and ceilings to hear more – sometimes half the night, they just won't let go. He has been free of COVID19 but still suffers from a regular Mystery Virus, producing flu-like symptoms, which he named after Peter Mandelson. He is writing an autobiography, full of the famous people who knew him, called <u>My Goodness, How I Roared!</u> and compiling a set of upbeat homilies called <u>Happy Talk</u>, tasks regularly interrupted by the tiresome Prodnose. He faces competition in the upbeat homily market from the Resident Mouse.

His entourage expands to include a poetic cockroach who claims to be the famous archy and a bridge-playing goldfish.

Footnotes are provided for references which may be obscure to non-UK readers.

16 March

My Mystery Virus, the one I named after Peter Mandelson[1], has departed, pro tem. I know he still prowls like the troops of Midian.

He continues to leave me, and medical science, baffled but in the present crisis caused by his Big Brother Covid I cannot ask the National Health Service to pay any more attention to him. He forces me to sleep, usually for two days at a time, sometimes longer. He sometimes throws in a headache and a cough. That has been the limit of his power. He robs me of the power to play cricket, to play the piano or to write more novels which nobody reads and more screenplays which nobody screens. These activities add almost nothing to the economy and not much more to society (especially the piano playing). More seriously, he shuts me out of family and social life, which has been a useful training for torpor and boredom during the four months' self-immolation which Boris Johnson, that unselfish patriot, has decreed for me.

---

[1] Labour politician, key influence on Tony Blair, who still evokes strong feelings (mostly antipathy) although out of office for ten years.

All in all, as a virus Mandelson is pretty small potatoes, as is his namesake.

17 March

The Times failed to publish my Angry Over70 letter. I shall give them one more day to recover their senses and then publish it here should they not.

Some other miscreant besides me has been panic-buying fresh limes near Rubato Towers. I was relying on them to get through my four months' quarantine. I may have rely on Plan B: Squire Haggard's method,[2] insensible from my stock of strong cordial waters.

18 March

The Times was still too wimpy to publish my letter: what happened to the Thunderer? Here it is.

---

[2] Squire Haggard was a superb, long-running parody by Michael Green of the diary of a wicked eighteenth-century English country squire. Typical entries rejoiced in evicting his tenants and then drinking himself insensible.

Sir,

The great majority of over-70s will doubtless obey the government's imminent demand to incarcerate themselves for four months.[3] But some will think themselves healthy and hygienic and young-enough looking to defy it, and one wonders how the measure will be enforced against them. The police will be too busy with serious crimes. Will we see self-appointed younger vigilantes on the streets demanding proof of age from suspects? Will people report sightings of their older neighbours in the forbidden outdoors? When detected and convicted how will these rogue oldies be punished – not, one hopes, in our already over-crowded prisons?

Yours sincerely,

Richard Heller (72)

---

[3] Appeared for a time as if government intended to force <u>all</u> over70s to stay at home for four months. Eventually took general power to lock down most of the population, with very limited forays out of home.

19 March

As world cricket shuts down, it is good to reflect that it has taken hold in Bhutan, whose economy measures Gross National Happiness. Two years ago the national team gained an emphatic victory over the Red Hordes of China. The setting for this national contest reminded me of many of the park matches I have played in, as did much of the Chinese bowling.

20 March

The full-size Tesco near Rubato Towers reminded me today of a branch of GUM in the old Soviet Union.[4] I found some Arabic yeast in one of the Middle Eastern stores nearby and am wondering if it will make only Arabic bread. Since Boris Johnson says the crisis will be over in 12 weeks, I bought enough limes for 24. Although I now have enough for survival Plan A of my four months'

---

[4] A dreary state department store which forced patrons to queue repeatedly for poorly made goods grudgingly served on production of the right form.

incarceration, I may yet go for Plan B with a Jereboam of margaritas.

I also bought some Arabic tuna. It is not dolphin-friendly. In fact, I could hear it mouthing "Who are you looking at, Flipper, you perv?" I am planning a book on Flipper and other famous performing dolphins of the past. It will be called Great Ex-Cetaceans. There will be a lot of sex in it because dolphins are sex-crazed, as much as sea urchins and with many more opportunities.

21 March

The first day of official spring and Rubato Towers is bathed in a pale pink glow. But there is a [blank] silence. [Punches cliché button]. Ah yes, an eerie silence. There are no birds tweeting but plenty of bores. And I realize that I have not heard any fornicating foxes for ages. Could it be that hungry hoarders are now eating all the junk food they normally throw away for them?

I have received an email from the Queen asking me to form a government of national salvation. Since there is no cricket, I will consider her invitation but I cannot understand why she needs all my bank account details.

22 March

Writers who never made any money are often described as enjoying a "succès d'estime". I'd rather have the money, although a drop of estime would be welcome too. However, there is an upside to living a writer's life in [blank] obscurity. [Punches cliché button. No response. Punches advanced cliché button.] Ah yes, indigent obscurity.

When and if my GP sends me the letter demanding self-incarcelation in Rubato Towers, it will hold no terrors. I shall miss my recent excursions to local Arabic shops (which appear to have better and nimbler supply chains than many household names) and the excitement of buying tinned goods with no English script in the hope that they will contain something like the illustration. Otherwise my routine of timewasting on Twitter, footling on Facebook, nestling into Netflix and naps between naps will be little affected.

Working from home, or more accurately avoiding it, has become a little easier during the crisis. The demands of hygiene are a perfect excuse to defer the awful moment, for any writer, of staring at a blank screen, and, in my case, the even more awful moment of reading the terrible opening paragraph I compose to fill it. ("To call this writer's work derivative would insult those he plagiarizes.") Instead, I can now spray-wash individually each of the bibelots, and scrub areas previously long abandoned to the mice.

Incidentally, the mice seem to have gone, even the homeless chap who became my lodger and introduced me to his chums, Terence Ratagain and Mousehole Proust (in 2017, a year of lost content.) What is the virus doing to animal life? I think we should be told.

23 March

Still no letter from my GP telling me to self-incarcelate for 12 weeks. He is under the correct impression that I am over 70 but the incorrect one that I have COPD. I have told him many times that my odd breathing has nothing to do with COPD but is the result of Stress, do you hear me, Stress, seriously STRESS, and it comes on worst when somebody tells me to relax. [Screams. A brief interlude.]

Anyway, I have prepared for incarcelation by choosing a book to read (not the Bible or Shakespeare) and eight gramophone records.[5]

Book: Camus La Peste. A bit obvious, but principally for the character ironically named Grand, a downtrodden clerk, who is perpetually writing a novel although it never gets beyond one sentence. Grand imagines himself submitting the

---

[5] The basic premise of a long-running popular radio programme, Desert Island Discs, in which Celebrities review their lives and choose eight sound recordings to illustrate them.

full manuscript to a publisher and being summoned to meet their entire board of directors. When he is ushered in, the chairman exclaims "Gentlemen, hats off! A genius!" I share this fantasy despite years of contrary evidence.

Records: Fats Waller Ain't Misbehaving. Duke Ellington Don't Get Around Much Any More. Frank Sinatra Don't Worry 'Bout Me (I Get Along). Roy Orbison Only The Lonely. The Beatles I Call Your Name (But You're Not There). The Beatles Eight Days A Week (Are Not Enough To Show You I Care). Traffic No Time To Live. And of course The Singing Walrus Wash Your Hands.

To encourage coronavirus lockdown, the government might repeat the famous World War 2 poster campaign as Careless Walks Cost Lives, with pastiches of original drawings by Fougasse. In place of eavesdropping Hitler one could put a stylized virus over subtext You Never Know Who's Lurking. Stay At Home. Just put this thought to Matt Hancock[6]. Any support welcome.

---

[6] The UK Health Secretary. Have played cricket with and against him.

Prodnose[7]: surely only older people remember those posters?

Myself: the very ones the government is trying to keep at home!

23 March bis

Suddenly I feel sorry for MPs.

Prodnose: Whatever for? [Cliché button goes into overdrive] Overpaid... waste of space... never done a proper job ... only out for themselves ... Know what I'd do with them all....? [Removed for legal reasons]

Myself: With so many constituents in lockdown they are going to receive shoals of extra emails

---

[7] A tiresome carping character I have stolen from the great humorist Beachcomber.

demanding action or at least the pretence of attention.

My own luckless Member, the indefatigable Neil Coyle, Labour, Bermondsey and Old Southwark (of course they barred me from living in Young Southwark with all the hipsters), has already had many pieces of my mind: on the fornicating foxes problem, on ranting preachers in local buses, on people who should be removed from any position of influence in the Labour party (94th volume in preparation), and on pressing international topics, including fish stocks in São Tomé e Príncipe. Neil took a strong stand on this matter, and is now urging our government to help STeP, and other small island countries, to quarantine themselves.

Writing to your MP is an even better way of avoiding work from home than washing all the dishrags or running the Socks Lonely Hearts Club. ("Sock, thick, gray, GSOH (Good Support Over Heel) would like to meet similar. Interests: cricket.") It makes you feel important and public-spirited.

MPs would not have so many emails and letters if Departments and official bodies knew how to answer them properly. When I was an underling in the civil service in the 1970s I spent much of my time answering letters <u>personally.</u> I had to read them and take care with the reply. A good reply would silence the correspondent, an unsatisfactory one would have him/her writing back to me, or worse still, be quoted in the House of Commons by a zealous MP. The ultimate nightmare was to be cited there in minute detail by the legendary basso Sir Tam Dalyell of the Binns[8]. "I have a letter to my constituent from a Mr Heller of the Department of Bubbleblowing. It is typed on Crown Watermark paper in single-spacing on one side only. The letter F is slightly out of alignment…"

Now it is very rare to get a signed letter from a Department. They are cranked out by anonymous Central Correspondence Units, I suspect without human agency, since I cannot believe that anyone

---

[8] As Tam Dalyell, Labour MP, a very punctilious interrogator in the House of Commons, especially during the Falklands War.

would actually want to work there. Does anyone get promoted from such a Unit? Certainly not for reading the letters. A dead giveaway in official replies is the sentence: "It may be helpful to explain the background to the government's decision to..." No, it isn't. The true meaning is "we don't care what you think about the government's decision to... and we are even less interested in your suggestion for a better alternative."

24 March

My junk email folder is usually full of Nigerians offering me untold riches, or else offers to enlarge an intimate part of my body or reduce all the others. Now it has been invaded by a *faux bonhomme* called William. Showering me with spurious wishes for my health, he offers to sell me face masks and protective clothing at a bargain price.

Get away with you! I suspect that your masks and clothing would disgrace a child's Halloween costume. If they were any good, I would want them to cover a health worker not a *bouche inutile* such as mine. *Bouche inutile* was a ruthless French military term for people who made no contribution to the nation's war-fighting capacity (sadly it included much of the French army in 1940). I think it might usefully be extended now to people who spread fake news about Covid19. President T Ronald Dump will know whom I mean.

A beautiful sunlit Day 4 of Spring over Rubato Towers. I greet it with a [blank] laugh. [Punches cliché button]. Of course, a hollow, mirthless laugh.

On such days in normal times, I would be outdoors purveying the zombie, the zamboni, the zipper, the zorker (continues page 94) to grateful recipients. A sunlit day without cricket to watch or play is an Imperial gallon of gall, and as Julius Caesar discovered, all gall is divided into three parts, resentment, rancour and rage.

No letter from GP. Joy! I can go out and scour local shops in search of a swede.

25 March

Another beautiful sunlit day: curse it and this entire cricketless spring. But we must see it through. Cricket will return, and sooner than Douglas Macarthur. Perhaps we should think of this time as an extended version of the shipping forecast which so often displaces Test Match Special during important passages of play. I wonder how they're getting on in Rockall, Malin and North Utsire?[9]

The combination of face masks and social distancing (should it not be antisocial or even counter-social distancing?) makes spoken conversation almost impossible. When one sees an acquaintance, one now limits oneself to a [blank] nod. [Punches cliché button.] Just so, a curt nod. At least it spares the embarrassment of having to remember the person's name.

---

[9] Exotic marine locations, known to most Britons only through the shipping forecast

These conditions would have messed up Plato no end. A limit of two people per symposium, forced to bellow philosophy at each other. "I said 'Love is born into every human being; it calls back the halves of our original nature together; it tries to make one out of two and heal the wound of human nature,' but let it pass, let it pass." The symposists might just as well get rat-arsed immediately[10], which is probably what happened in the first place.

26 March

Another vile, sunny day…

Prodnose: Enough! You have done this one to death.

Myself: Very well. But when cricket is restored, you can bet that the weather will shift to continuous deluge.

---

[10] Rat-arsed: British slang for seriously drunk, particularly if intentional.

Britain's zoos are being forced to close, which must represent a major loss of income. I am worried by the impact of the crisis on all their inmates: hundreds of species each with different complex needs for food, habitat maintenance and specialist care and medical attention. During the siege of Paris in 1870-71 they ate most of the zoo inmates, which is why old editions of Larousse Gastronomique carry recipes for lion and bear. This should not happen again, since the trade in exotic wildlife as foodstuffs might well have promoted the virus in the first place. But zoo inmates could be at risk from disruption of their food supplies: they might perish naturally or have to be culled.

This would have profound political implications. One remembers Tony Blair in the foot-and-mouth crisis of 2001 claiming credit for the reprieve of Phoenix, the cute calf. Boris Johnson might not survive the avoidable death of a panda. One predicts the screaming tabloid story: PAND – EMIC! Horror as adorable Ly-Chee starves to death".

If there were a threat to pandas' food supply, you could count on thousands of well-meaning people donating their old bamboo furniture, alas, to Noah Vail.

27 March

Rubato Towers saw the unwelcome return of two fornicating foxes. They were at it like dolphins or sea urchins. For length and volume, their screeches outdid our collective cheers for the NHS workers[11]. I reached for my usual ammunition (one of my books) but finally they decided they had had enough before I could throw it.

---

[11] The evening of 26 March saw a mass cheer for all NHS workers, the first of a regular series.

A screeching night in store

One upside of the crisis: my weight has dipped below 11 stone (70 kilos) for the first time since my soccer-playing days. Since you ask, I was a specialist decoy runner, making space for others. I was successful in this role for long periods in the game until the opposition realized that none of my team would ever pass to me. Several pairs of familiar trousers have cascaded to the ground like

Brian Rix's at the old Whitehall theatre[12]. As well that I am not going out in them to meet my public.

28 March

Barely a week of lockdown and millions of people are pining for the office to get away from their families and cats. They have discovered painfully that they are not actually needed at their office and some, still more painfully, that they are not needed at all.

Most offices are otiose. The revelation will cause many ugly office developments to founder after the crisis. Heh-heh. Most of the activity in offices generates no useful output or any contribution to public welfare.

This was discovered years ago by the great cartoonist Frank Dickens, who drew Bristow, the

---

[12] Brian Rix, a comic actor, later a life peer, who starred in many traditional British "Whitehall farces" in which his trousers would fall down. His timing for this was always impeccable.

definitive account of office life anywhere. It ran in the London <u>Evening Standard</u> for over fifty years.

Devotees can instantly recall all the cast. The hero, Bristow, is a downtrodden but crafty buying clerk in the giant Chester-Perry organization, housed in the gigantic building of the same name. His boss is the irascible martinet Fudge, who rarely says anything more than **GET ON WITH YOUR WORK!** in block caps. Bristow has constant but futile dreams of escape. He pines for an occasional visitor, the gorgeous Miss Pretty of Kleenaphone, studies a book called <u>Brain Surgery For Beginners</u> and is constantly rewriting a thick novel called <u>Living Death In The Buying Department.</u> (I still have a plot for this novel myself, and the longest and most bibulous lunch of my career was in Joe Allen's with Frank Dickens to discuss it.)[13]

Other supporting characters include smooth Sampson of Sales, astonishingly rude Peterson of

---

[13] Celebrity-haunted American restaurant in London's theatreland, with fine selection of cocktails

Public Relations, sycophantic Hickford, editor of the Chester-Perry house journal, the pretentious but incompetent canteen chef Gordon Blue, the tea ladies, some still recovering from the Great Tea Trolley Disaster of 1967, Bristow's only friend the pigeon.... [*That's enough characters. Ed.*] Anyway, Dickens created this complete office world, overflowing with drama, over 51 years without ever revealing what the Chester-Perry organization actually produced.

Although many redundant offices will disappear after the crisis, there is scope to re-invent them as members' clubs for people who want to get away from home. Already some offices seem to be more like leisure centres, with ping-pong, table football, climbing walls, exercise classes, exciting ethnic finger food and dress-as-you-like. That's all very well for young creative types, but older workers will need something more like the Chester-Perry building in their simulated office club. It must offer drabness, drudgery and dread, such as Bristow endured daily, because perversely this will give its inmates a sense of importance (this is what I have to endure). It is vital that inmates put on different, uncomfortable clothes before they go there (in Bristow's case, the forgotten clerical uniform of striped trousers, black jacket and bowler hat.)

MPs and peers confirm my theory. Although they could easily work remotely, they insist on travelling to premises which are shockingly inconvenient even after the rest of us pay for expensive refurbishments. Why? Because it makes them feel important. And they will go back there, as if nothing had happened, after the crisis.

Although I have long worked "from" home (revealing preposition, suggesting disassociation) I make a point of changing for work. If I am attempting some light verse I change into the suit and shirt I picked up in Florida, which Jeeves would have burnt had it been purchased by Bertie. For angry pieces or letters, a loud three-piece number with a clashing tie. For tiresome correspondence with the VAT man, the grubby tracksuit bottoms snatched from a skip.

29 March

Loo roll reappeared yesterday in some local shops. The once-empty streets were lined with long eager queues, sprawling far beyond the lines of distancing tape put down by the shopkeepers. Strong silent men and women were seen to shed strong, silent tears and not a few even burst into song. Total strangers ~~embraced passionately in doorways~~ gave each other a shy grin across the appropriate interval. I noticed a detachment of riot police, in preparation for the re-appearance of eggs.

When and if all the crisis is over, will it be mythologized to become another Finest Hour like the Blitz? Will we be asked to remember only the heroic NHS workers, the onrush of volunteers, the sudden acts of kindness by neighbours and to forget all the negative, selfish behaviours, the bursts of hatred they provoked in conventional and social media and the [blank] legislation [punches cliché button] of course, draconian legislation introduced to control them? If the new Finest Hour myth takes hold, will the fake Churchill in charge of our affairs be as revered as the real one?

30 March

We have all become very neighbourly in Rubato Towers and I am doing my bit for everyone by increasing my output of cocktail melodies at the piano. One of the neighbours paid me a very nice compliment: "When I hear you playing a tune, it's like hearing it for the first time." It's good to think I can connect people to their past. As Luke Upward so aptly put it: "memory is a cosy on the teapot of time." That said, I cannot help imagining how rocky a past my neighbour must have undergone to hear piano playing like mine before. I can recall only one pianist who was anything like me, in a dive in Tirana, just after the ultimate fall of Communism in 1992, trying to pick out the fleeting melodies he had heard on a secret radio, in peril of his life, across the airwaves over the Adriatic from Bari. I did my best to help him but he could not follow my chromatic progressions.

The bar was a product of the brief economic explosion of post-Communist Albania, which produced the famous headline TIRANA BOOM

TODAY. I had to leave that bar in a hurry, not because of the piano but because smoking seemed to be compulsory. One of the rare bits of luck in my life was to discover that I hated smoking once I had left school and it was no longer daring and forbidden.

The Times Letter Editor has again failed to publish the letter I sent and this one was not even angry. If this continues I shall be compelled to write him/her a sharp letter.

31 March

The Times has ignored my letter again, in spite of the closing flattery, so here it is.

The Editor
The Times

Sir,

The Times reported yesterday that over 700,000 people have volunteered to help the NHS through the coronavirus crisis. Some might usefully be enlisted by the Department of Health itself, to give an intelligent first response to the shoals of additional letters and emails which must have poured into it. These volunteers could flag up potentially useful suggestions for coping with the crisis, of which many will almost certainly be submitted by regular correspondents of The Times.

I am looking for a better outlet. I like the sound of the British Goat Society Journal, which promises not only expert advice but also articles of more general interest: about goatkeepers at home and goatkeeping ideas as well as a few more light hearted articles. There is an advertisement section, as well as "letters to the editor". It might become my "goat-to" publication but it seems to have ceased publication in 2014.

1 April

The British Goat Society Journal may be one with Nineveh and Tyre but the Journal of Molluscan Studies is in fine fettle, or should that be cuttle?

Anyway, I have been studying its content to see if it might accept any of my stuff and have been enjoying one of its most-read articles "Factors Contributing To Spatial Heterogeneity In The Abundance Of The Common Periwinkle".

One of my public caught up with my recent reference to my football career and asked me about its highlights. This will not take long.

In a very elastic sense I played two internationals for Brazil in the 1970s – guesting in London's Regent's Park for a team drawn from their embassy. My role in the games was simple, get the ball somehow and give it at once to the nearest Brazilian, even the eleven-year-old. We won both matches.

I was more prominent in another match for my regular weekend side. Our captain had an earthy Anglo-Saxon vocabulary, used loudly and frequently. Early in the match I saw the referee about to book him and called out in the nick of time. "Ref! I don't think you understand. Our captain was not swearing, he was calling me for a pass. My name is F***ov. I come from a Bulgarian family, the F***ovs of Plovdiv." The ref seemed to believe this: at any rate he put the book away. Our captain stayed out of trouble and was able to express himself quite freely. I had to play as F***ov for the rest of the match. I actually saw much more of the ball than usual.

I had an utterly unsuitable football role model when I was a boy, someone I could never remotely imitate on the field. It was the bandy-legged Brazilian genius Garrincha, often rated the greatest dribbler of all time. He helped to win Brazil's first two World Cups. In matches, if he thought he had not beaten his full-back artistically enough he would take the ball back to the half-way line and do it all over again. Garrincha's off-field life was far more turbulent than George Best's. He died young and poor and wrecked by injury and cheap alcohol. But in his day he was known as "the joy of the people." What a wonderful title to earn from any sporting life, from any life…

Prodnose: You're blubbing. No one knows you're a softie at heart.

Myself: Silence when you're talking to me! Remix this jigger, emphasizing the tequila and this time using the proper Triple Sec instead of Cointreau.

2 April

Private Eye printed my letter pointing out that if Elizabeth Warren became the Democrats' choice of running-mate it would set up an epic, Tolstoyan Vice-Presidential debate of Warren Pence. Most gratifying but not compensation enough for rejection by The Times. I continued to research the Journal of Molluscan Studies as a possible outlet and found another gripping read: "First evidence of introgressive hybridization of apple snails (*Pomacea* spp.) in their native range." Unfortunately I know nothing about molluscs except those I've seen on a plate. Somehow I don't think the Journal will publish my recipes for scallops.

3 April

Next to cricket, the London Library is my prime resource for wasting time and it is now closed for the duration. It houses an astonishing collection of books, many of them rare, and you can take them home as easily as books from the old Boots lending libraries.[14] They are sometimes hard to locate because of its idiosyncratic Victorian cataloguing system. It is way more exciting than boring old Dewey-Decimal but takes some getting used to: for example, books on Iraq are still housed under its ancient name of Mesopotamia. Because of the system, Cricket is next door to Cremation, making it the ideal place to find a book on the Ashes. [Roars.]

The Library has a great number of out-of-print editions of Rex Stout, creator of the rotund and orotund detective Nero Wolfe. He was a favourite of P G Wodehouse. and in case you missed it, my

---

[14] Boots the chemist had a library service until at least the Fifties. I can remember the weekly ritual of changing Library books there. You can still find their editions of mainstream fiction in secondhand shops, with a little hole punched in the cover.

tribute to him in the PG Wodehouse Society journal.

http://www.richardheller.co.uk/?s=Rex+Stout And now when I need them most all those Stouts are unobtainable. [Screams]. Self-isolation is the time to go back to all those Great Novels you meant to read and discover why you never read them in the first place. Starting with Marcel f***ing Proust (pardon my French). There was a popular T-shirt in the Sixties saying "Marcel Proust was a yente."[15] I wonder if they still make it.

Apart from valuable books, the London Library has all my novels. I gave them, the latest five years ago. I did the same to the wonderful Sind Club in Karachi and they put them in a special cabinet in their library. Flattering, but also, I think, carrying a hidden message to members: we got stuck with these, and you don't actually actually have to read them...

---

[15] Yiddish: an endlessly chattering woman.

Prodnose: You're paranoid.

Myself: With good reason!

Anyway, the London Library put my novels in the regular fiction collection next to the more famous non-relative Joseph. There I made the mortifying but familiar discovery that no one had ever borrowed them. I made a similar discovery with my first cricket novel on a repeat visit to the Cricket Club of India library, to whom I had presented it four years previously, and rectified the omission by borrowing it myself as a guest to get the first return date stamped in the virgin issue slip. I was too embarrassed to do this at the London Library where they sort of know me. I imagined myself furtively presenting my novel at the Issue Desk, the librarian comparing the author's name on the book with the identical name on my library card, the sad, pitying smile, the mocking gossip at the next coffee break. So I found another apparently unborrowed author and tried to form a mutual assistance pact: if I borrow your novel will you borrow mine? He turned me down in something of a huff, so I am forming a society of Readers of Readerless Novels on the model of that splendid British institution Friends of Friendless Churches. I should not repine. I found near me among the Hs a novel that had not been borrowed in nearly a hundred years since its acquisition. It was called The Plowers by Agnes Grozier Herbertson[16]. I borrowed it at once, and it is not half bad. If the world gets that far, my heartfelt thanks to my first posthumous borrower in 2120.

4 April

I wonder if they will make coronavirus movies, with special rules on social distancing for the lovers. One remembers the old Hays Office which

---

[16] Better known as a poet. Her Great War poems, Airman RFC and The Seed Merchant's Son, have been set as texts in English exams for teenagers.

governed American movies in their greatest era, and their rule that two people on a bed had to have one foot on the floor. Each. [Rushes to piano. Thump-thump-thump-thump. Sings.]

A fine romance with no clinches
A fine romance at 78.7 inches
We should be making each other feel desirous
But we've been kept apart by this blasted virus.
A fine romance, with no hugging
If this is romance I'd rather have a mugging
We're spaced out like a couple of desert plants
Our life is a set of can'ts
This is a fine romance.

Prodnose: Some of the stresses are wrong.

Myself: What do you know of stress, you torpid turnip! [Screams]. [17]

---

[17] Original lyrics by Dorothy Fields music by Jerome Kern.

5 April

My advance copy of Wisden Cricketers Almanack failed to arrive but I did get a letter from Boris Johnson, which was no compensation. Needless to say, it was no reply to any of the letters I have sent him since he became Prime Minister, even the one which was genuinely encouraging. It was the one telling everyone to stay at home except when they are allowed to leave home or go to work.

A whiff of self-justification sometimes broke through it, as from a forgotten piece of cheese and an ominous reminder that the police will issue fines to rule-breakers and disperse gatherings with no further process. But what stuck in my [punches advanced cliché button] craw was the claim that with our "great British spirit" we will beat coronavirus. Boris seems to have forgotten that there are over six million non-British people in our country (I know he wants fewer of them). Many are essential to our health and care services and all those millions need to be enlisted in the struggle. A moment's thought might have removed the reference to British and produced a universal human appeal which might be better suited to fighting a global pandemic. Is this carping?

Prodnose: Yes.

Myself: Then I shall carp. We all paid for that letter. I have a master's licence from the Nitpickers Institute and am the original of the moaning minnies denounced all those years ago by Harold Wilson.[18]

<u>5 April (bis)</u>

By popular request I have added a second verse to the romantic virus number. I know the stresses are difficult and don't tell me I wasted two ants

---
[18] British Labour Prime Minister 1964-70 and 1974-76

rhymes... Oddly enough, it's a little closer in spirit to the original by Dorothy Fields and Jerome Kern.

A fine romance with no clinches
A fine romance at 78.7 inches
We should be making each other feel desirous
But we've been kept apart by this blasted virus.
A fine romance, with no hugging
If this is romance I'd rather have a mugging
We're spaced out like a couple of desert plants
Our life is a set of can'ts
This is a fine romance.

A fine romance, with no dances
And no close-ups but distant glances:
We used to kick and twirl like a Broadway chorus
But now we keep apart like two lovesick walrus.
A fine romance, my good fellow,
With no love songs unless we bellow.
A fleeting kiss is simply too great a chance,
When we're locked in durance,
This is a fine romance.

<u>6 April</u>

I am bowled over by the Queen's message. So are many diehard Republicans such as Alastair Campbell. What a contrast to the phoney fustian of Boris Johnson's letter. And to Donald Trump. [Pauses to enjoy Swiss cough sweet.] "A frightened, hollow man who has been found out, who can no longer be protected by his bodyguard of lies, a Commander-in-Chief who cannot even command himself, let alone preserve and protect the United States."

The message was superbly crafted (by whom, I wonder, one person or a team? Peerages all round) and immaculately delivered. Her Majesty has her 94th birthday soon. (The real one: 21 April. She is the only British sovereign to be born in a house with a number. 17 Bruton Street, Mayfair, am I right, sir, am I right, now of all things a Chinese restaurant.) I shall send her my latest book. No, that's stingy. I shall give her the lot. I email the Royal Household to arrange for collection and delivery.

I have been having some minor eye trouble which makes it hard to wear my contact lenses, including the pair I commissioned for batting which the oculist focused on 20 yards (futile, of course, one won't see the ball any better if one never watches the thing in the first place.) One consequence is that I now find it hard to read the chords in the fakebook of the cocktail melodies I play for the neighbours on the piano.

Prodnose: And that makes a difference?

Myself: One needs a target area. I wonder if anyone's invented a Satnav for shortsighted pianists? A little voice that could whisper into one ear "F Minor 7, then at the next bar turn left to B flat seven for two beats and then make a sharp right to E flat. You have now reached your destination." It might render my performances troppo lento e maestoso.

An email pings back from some Royal flunkey called Sir Cyril Screamer, Rouge Drag On Extraordinary. He thanks me on behalf of Her Majesty, but she is unselfishly declining all gifts from her subjects and urges me instead to give my books to the neighbours. Fool! They won't take any more.

7 April

My advance copy of Wisden Cricketer's Almanack has finally arrived and I may be gone for some time.

[Later, page 845 or so]. Briefly interrupting perusal of Wisden and anxious search for progress of Bhutan cricket in 2019, to express **best wishes** to Boris Johnson for a speedy recovery[19]. I know that he follows my stuff although he never replies to my letters, so he will realize that he is finally out of danger when he reads my next volley of irony, insult and invective. A few real zingers in waiting.

---

[19] He went down with the COVID virus.

<u>8 April</u>

I woke up sleepless again. [Long pause. Worries. Is this a piece of elegantly simple paradox? Or destined for deserved taunting in Pseuds Corner? Pretencioso? Mi? Dozes off again.]

[Later]. As I was saying… I woke up after a long nominal sleep feeling as tired as when I started. This was one of the common symptoms of my obnoxious visitor Mandelson the Mystery Virus, whom I had thought too ashamed to return in the time of his big brother Covid. If it be Mandelson again [grammer] I care even less now that the new Wisden has arrived. I cannot find Bhutan but there is a sparkling paragraph about cricket in Guam. For devotees, it holds the same power to remove anxiety as Whiffle's <u>Care Of The Pig</u> held over Lord Emsworth.

A return to sleep is impossible. Since the crisis, Rubato Towers has become rural rather than urban and the birds make so much racket in the early morning that one pines for the heavy lorries of old. Will continue these stray notes for my public.

A curious by-product of the crisis is the reappearance of the acronym PPE which I read in a previous life at Oxford, although in my case it stood for Poker, Pantomime and Erratics (the name of our social cricket club, for non-initiates). It makes me proud of the MA I paid for a few years later, on a false rumour that Oxford was about to convert it into a real degree.[20] As if the University could afford to give up such an easy money-raiser. One might as well expect the political parties to give up the sale of honours. It would be nice if just this once they held off and confined the next list to people who had given genuine service to the nation in the crisis.

---

[20] Oxford University alumni may still make a small payment to upgrade a BA into an MA, after an interval, without doing any further work for it.

8 April (bis)

I must apologize for an error in the previous posting. "Pretencioso? Mi?" should of course have read "¿Pretencioso? ¿Mi?"

9 April (Maundy Thursday, named, I believe, after Maundy Gregory, the only man to be jailed for selling honours and titles, and inventor of Maundy money).

So our country is now in the hands of Dominic Raab, who was the sixth choice for leader by his party's MPs in the last Parliament. No offence but I'd rather have the late Raab Buttler. Or his distant cousin Jos[21], who isn't doing much at the moment. Or Peter Raabit. Or Raabit from Winnie-the-Pooh, or any of his friends and relations, including the beetle Henry Small. Or why not the Easter Bunny, who will be free this weekend, as only the New

---
[21] Jos Buttler is an England cricketer

Zealand Prime Minister, Jacinda Ardern, had the acuity to notice?

This is a dangerous time for the Raab we've got. There is no apparent end of lockdown and people are vexed and frustrated. Familiar goods have returned to the shops and there is no thrill any more in detecting loo roll or celeriac, or in devising exotic recipes for pilchards[22] with dried apricots, to make use of forgotten items in store cupboards. Plans to use the time for self-improvement have long been abandoned. Great novels pile up unread beside settees, language courses have stopped at lesson 3 (although I can now say "¡Caramba! El postillón ha sido alcanzado por un rayo" should the need arise)[23], hectoring fitness videos have been silenced as have wheedling meditation gurus.

---

[22] A depressing oily canned fish: I am not aware if it is consumed anywhere except the UK.
[23] Spanish for "Good lord! The postillion has been struck by lightning", a probably apochryphal useless sentence from Victorian language guides.

People have stopped shaving or flossing and sartorial standards at home are making a vertiginous descent: even I no longer change my tie to compose light verse.

I warned the government some time ago about the peril to zoo animals in the crisis and now poor Nadia the tiger has caught the Covid virus in the Bronx Zoo in New York. As a caretaker leader, Raabit could not survive such a development here. He will probably order mass testing for all our zoo creatures, or at least the cute ones.

9 April (bis)

"It was going to be one of Raabit's busy days. As soon as he woke up he felt important, as if everything depended upon him. It was just the day for Organizing Something, or for Writing a Notice Signed Raabit, or for Seeing What Everybody Else Thought About It".

10 April

Happy Easter to all! This year I shall much miss my normal routine of coming off the bench as a substitute Easter Bunny for my grandchildren. Easter eggs have been selling as normal near Rubato Towers, and, I gather, elsewhere. One feels for all those parents who have been cooped up indoors for days with their children and will now have to cope with the coopees having a massive sugar rush. Or will the police be swooping on illicit outdoor egg hunts? We need a statement on this from the Home Secretary, Priti Patel, but she has been hidden too well by the real Easter Bunny.

Boris Johnson is on the mend. The Sun greets this event with a headline that crosses the frontier between sycophancy and blasphemy: "Now it really is a Good Friday!" I dread to think of its headline should Boris get up on Sunday and have a little walk. If it keeps up this sort of stuff, the Sun will lose its reputation as a serious newspaper.

Saturation reporting of Boris Johnson, but no further news of Nadia, the stricken tiger at the Bronx Zoo. Not my idea of balanced coverage.

11 April

Boris Johnson has taken a short walk. Wake up, the Sun! Where's your story: "on the second day he rose again"?

No UK coverage of the wonderful news that Nadia the tiger is recovering from the virus. When our media had standards Nadia would have had non-stop attention, as did poor Victor the giraffe in 1977. Victor, an inmate of Marwell Zoo near Winchester, collapsed while attempting to mate one of his companions (female, I understand, although the other giraffe has never been identified and many gay giraffes were still in the closet in that era, as witness the contemporary Jeremy Thorpe scandal). A collapse with splayed legs is a terrible event for a giraffe and daily attempts were made to induce Victor to rise, including his favourite food just out of reach and recorded love calls from the mysterious "other". They were reported in detail by all media, especially on BBC Two's television news by the legendary Peter Woods. Like his great contemporary Reginald Bosanquet, he found it helpful to take a bracing tot before reading the news. As the days passed and each attempt to raise Victor failed, Peter Woods became more and more emotionally involved in the story. Finally he had to read the terrible news that Victor had died during the last desperate attempt to haul him up with a winch. He was almost choked with stifled tears, but got through it gallantly. He ended the bulletin: "And now here is the weather – the weather Victor will never see."

I will try to organize a mass roar for Nadia when her recovery is complete. What people do about Boris Johnson is a matter entirely for them, so long as it remains within the confines of law and does not frighten a giraffe.

12 April (My first Mastermind subject Harry Truman became President on this day in 1945)

Nadia the tiger is better today. She is back on her food and managed to eat a tourist who had broken the lockdown rules. (I made that up, but Nadia really is improving.)

A double calamity for the neighbours. My piano has gone out of tune…

Prodnose: How…

Myself: Silence that turgid tired trope which is [punches cliché button] long past its sell-by date. I suppose so, although sell-by dates are being widely ignored amid the shortages of the crisis. In defiance of its label, many a sagging courgette has been purchased and consumed…

Prodnose (sings): Courgettes, I've had a few…

Myself (amazed): Good grief, the drudge has learnt something from me. My life's work is not in vain.

The other calamity is the electronic keyboard. The notes no longer cut off but sustain indefinitely and merge into one hideous clashing chord...

Prodnose: And the difference is?...

Myself (treating him with lofty ignoral)[24] The out-of-tune piano removes the elusive joy that I have played something which coincides with the composer's intentions. And it has wrecked my new movie script which I had intended to set here in Rubato Towers. Read it here and guess which part I had written for myself.

A Murder Of Note   by   Richard Heller

The best screenplay what I have written this week. Available to investors as a fun way to make a tax loss.

---

[24] Ignoral is a splendid word invented by George Brown, Labour's bibulous Deputy Leader in the 1960s. Confronted at a press conference with allegations about his behaviour at a party he replied "I'm treating them with ignoral."

Xander (have always liked names beginning with X) is a handsome young pianist of extraordinary talent. He is swindled out of his inheritance by his evil cousin Coron (I don't think viruses can sue.) Coron moves into their dead great-uncle's spacious apartment, with not only the priceless bibelots but worse still, the unique Steinway piano which had once belonged to the crooked composer, Shyster Kovich. In his, his (punches cliché button) garret, of course, poor heroes like Xander always live in a garret, although they don't come on the market very often these days, certainly not at a price poor heroes can afford, anyway delighting the passing pigeons with scintillating arpeggios on his barely functional upright, Xander dreams of revenge. He has an inspiration and it is marked by a thick dramatic chord of D over E.

Xander assumes an impenetrable disguise. He secures employment as Coron's personal assistant. Stoically he squeezes Coron's toothpaste, cuts crusts off his sandwiches and roars at his jokes. The worst of his ordeal is to listen to Coron at the piano, a Les Dawson[25] without the talent. Such is his musical ability that he can recognize when Coron has reached the finale, and applauds wildly, scattering murmured compliments about "the interesting tempi, and so many of them". Not recognizing his cousin, Coron laps up the appreciation.

Xander endures. He has a carefully prepared alibi. At the right moment he batters Coron to death with a former candelabra of Liberace's. To sustain the alibi, Xander must pretend to be Coron at the piano for half an hour. But the effort is too much for him. After 32 bars he slides into the scintillating repertoire which delighted the pigeons.

Nonetheless his alibi seems to succeed. The police are ready to give up on the case as a murder by persons unknown. But one feature of the neighbours' evidence puzzles the great private detective … Anyone but Hercule Poirot. Has no one noticed what a klutz he is? The Library is always littered with more corpses than the end of

---

[25] British comedian and accomplished pianist who pretended successfully to be an awful one

Hamlet before he says "Ow eez it, mon cher
Aysteengs, that I have been so blind?" and names
the killer. The same for Miss bloody Marple.

Anyway, not-Hercule-Poirot notices that the
neighbours all testify that at bar 33 of his last
performance Coron suddenly played a lot better. It
is the clue not-H-P needs. He or she (let's see who's
available and for how much?) uncovers the secret
of Xander and his plot. He has betrayed himself by
his musical standards.

In the last scene we see him in solitary confinement
on Death Row. He has been allowed a piano in his
cell and is delighting a lonely sparrow with his
cadenzas. (Get leftover footage from Birdman Of
Alcatraz.)

12 April (bis)

The neighbours' torment is set to endure
indefinitely. This absurd government has ruled that
piano tuning is not an essential occupation. We are
back in the darkest days of the last war. I am
reminded of the poor old Duke of Devonshire,

when he was asked to release staff at Chatsworth House for essential war work. When they demanded one of his special French pastry chefs he said plaintively: "Mayn't a chap have a biscuit?"

If the crisis continues we may become like Pakistan. There are many beautiful pianos there but the art of piano tuning has all but disappeared. It may simply be lack of demand but perhaps it is some sort of post-colonial protest against Western intervals. At any rate, the even-tempered clavier has given way to the bad-tempered listener. I have warned my Pakistani friends that on my next visit, post-crisis, I shall be taking up the Pakistani harmonium. My favourite Pakistani cricketer from the early age was a notable performer, the gifted but [punches cliché button], that's it, mercurial, gifted-but people are invariably mercurial, Prince Aslam.

12 April (ter)

Fortunately, before the double failure of the piano and the keyboard, I was able to complete this song.

I hope it will find a market with punters worldwide.

A Horse With No Chance by Richard Heller (after America)

It is of course inspired by the rock classic A Horse With No Name by America. Check this brilliant rendition by a self-isolating couple. https://twitter.com/americaband/status/1241782311269457920 The long-haired lady was very brave to play a horse's ass, in the face of such stiff daily competition from Donald Trump. Pedant's note: names of horses in second verse are from the "Fugue For Tinhorns" in Guys And Dolls.

There are quite a few other parodies of the song and I have sent mine to the composer, Dewey Bunnell, who seems to be a sporting sort of cove and turns out to have born in Harrogate.[26]

---

[26] An English spa town.

My journey began in the OTB [*or betting shop for UK*]
I was glad to get out of the rain.
I saw runners and riders on all kind of screens
And I thought that my luck might change.

The first horse I saw was called Paul Revere
But they told me he didn't like mud,
Then I took a shine to one called Valentine
But some guy said that he was a dud.

So I put all my money on a horse with no chance,
I can't even remember his name:
His rider felt all kinds of shame
To be mounted on something so lame.

La la la-la-la-la
La la ... Lose

La la la-la-la-la
La la ... Lose.

I was staring hard at the TV screen
As they opened the starting gate

And I looked for my horse in the spray of mud
But it gave me a very long wait.

And then I got all excited
When my horse took second place
But when I tried to collect all my dreams were wrecked
Because he'd started in the previous race.

I'd put all my money on a horse with no chance
I can't even remember his name
His rider said that he wasn't to blame:
He was mounted on something so lame.

La la la-la-la-la
La la ... Lose.

La la la-la-la-la
La la ... Lose.

Long slow fade out. Like the horse.

13 April

Yesterday's song, <u>A Horse With No Chance,</u> derives from my unbroken record of failure on the turf. Some years ago, during the great horsemeat scandal, I saw one of my selections overtaken by a hamburger. And it wasn't even from a fast-food joint. I suggested more than once to leading bookmakers that they introduce a losing accumulator bet, to pay out when one had selected five or more horses which were strangers to place money. They told that it would threaten the purity of the turf to offer bets on horses to lose. Pity. I'd have made a fortune as a tipster.

With a cruel irony, Rubato Towers has received a list of small local retailers at exactly the moment when we are not allowed to go out and support them. I would definitely patronize the Eritrean curtainmaker but our increasingly tyrannical government has ruled that Eritrean curtains are not an essential item.

Rubato Towers gets more rural every day. Two abandoned vehicles in the car park have acquired a thick layer of moss and are becoming a nature reserve. One was being used as a sun lounger by a resident fox, recovering after an especially long night of fornication. I reached for my pearl-handled revolver (in the world of cliché, retro division, revolvers are always pearl-handled, in contrast to automatics, which are always snub-nosed. Incidentally, Camus means "snub-nosed" in English. I don't think he would have got published as Albert Snubnose) but then I remembered some advice from my MP, the indefatigable Neil Coyle. It is now against the law to kill a fox, except, and only in self-defence, by clubbing it to death. It gives a whole new meaning to going out clubbing.

At the Bronx zoo, Nadia the tiger continues to recover but they are trying to trace all her contacts. That really should not be too difficult for a zoo tiger, but perhaps Nadia was a real party animal.

14 April

My new store-cupboard recipe for pilchards with dried apricots was not a success. Nor was beef jerky with crushed Cheeselets.[27]

I have had to substitute housework for cricket as my main exercise and it is far more energetic.

The Resident Mouse (for he is back): What, the way you do housework?

Myself: You have not seen the way I do cricket. Housework of any kind is fierce on calories. I am certain that someone has produced a housework fitness video, with the usual booming music and the even more booming voice: "Dust to the left and dust to the right and now stretch right up to the hanging lampshade!" A small tip for increasing the exercise value: buy a rotten secondhand vacuum cleaner from a charity shop, so you have to do carpets twice or even thrice in a rage.

---

[27] Small cheesy crackers.

The combination of a new diet and a new exercise régime has caused more and more regular trousers to plummet to the ground. I could model for my idol Beachcomber's invention of Bracerot, a product designed to stop war by causing whole armies to lose their uniform trousers on the battlefield. Kindly neighbours have bought essential supplies of limes and lentils for me, otherwise I might have been forced to disappoint my public by leaving Rubato Towers in tracksuit bottoms.

Nadia the tiger is out of danger but one of my younger grandchildren has caused me to worry about Spongebob Squarepants and his chums. Can molluscs get the virus? I turned to the Journal of Molluscan Studies, but it did not supply an answer. I know it is very thorough and it would be far too soon to have any research peer-reviewed. I did enjoy its sparkling piece on "Assessing the diet of octopuses: traditional techniques and the stable isotopes approach." It was good to see the right plural of "octopus". The form "octopi" is simply wrong and the correct "octopodes" is too pedantic, even for me. The <u>Journal of Molluscan Studies</u> must be regarded as the ultimate arbiter.

15 April

In spite of the frustrations of lockdown there is a very stimulating atmosphere at Rubato Towers. Quite literally: we are enjoying the unfamiliar sensation of breathing fresh air.

It has inspired me to start another major literary work. But instead of another novel, I shall be writing my autobiography instead. There will not be much difference because all autobiography is fiction. (Discuss, with examples. This will be 60 per cent of your grade.) I felt that I owed it to a grateful posterity since quite a few famous people have met me, although not all at the same time, including Nelson Mandela, Bill Clinton, Garry Sobers, Howard Marks, Happy Fanny Fields, the great vaudeville artiste, and the Wali of Tangier. (The one who went AWOL for a while and inspired the Where's Wali? series of books.)

As I may have mentioned, my autobiography will be titled <u>My Goodness, How I Roared!</u> It will take the form of Mr Pooter's narrative, in which events are sandwiched between his very best jests. But whereas his are greeted with collective roars, my jests get one only from me. Like the last one.

I will have a problem writing about nearly all the famous people. Even without recordings or notes, I can remember well everything I said to them, but have almost no recollection of what, if anything, they said to me. I must make a confession. I had a similar problem with many Celebrities I interviewed for my old newspaper <u>The Mail On Sunday.</u> My recorder or notes would be full of sparkling material from me and muttered mediocrity or monosyllables from the Celebrity. To get the stuff into the paper, I regularly transferred some of my very best gems to the Celebrity. None of them ever objected afterwards, and I trust that the famous people will not protest when I do this to them in my autobiography, especially the ones who are deceased.

In fairness to me, there was a football correspondent, it might have been the great Brian Glanville, who used a similar technique to get good copy from the taciturn Alf Ramsey, England's World Cup winning manager. He would ask Ramsey very long questions: "Alf, do you think the Italians will play a modern catenaccio with rotating sweepers and a false number 10 in the space behind the hole?" If Alf mumbled anything like assent, our man was away: "Alf told me he was preparing for the Italians to play a modern catenaccio with rotating sweepers…"

It occurs to me that rotating sweepers are more usually seen in ice hockey before the match. My goodness, how I roared!

16 April

The fornicating foxes tested some new positions last night. I had finally dozed off after the last screech when I was almost immediately woken by the dustmen calling at Rubato Towers. I know that these days one is expected to use the gender-neutral euphemism sanitation engineers, but I have never seen a dustlady in the crew. Is there still a glass ceiling in garbage? I have the impression that our bins are being emptied more often in the crisis. True or not, Britain's unsung sanitation engineers are another frontline service against the virus and they deserve a burst of the public clapping which everyone seems to enjoy.

In preparation for my long-awaited autobiography I assembled a few of my very best jests, and of course in no time I was roaring again. Some kindly neighbours came to check whether lockdown had driven me to hysterics and I knew it was serious when the Resident Mouse begged me to play the piano instead.

I hate to give away too much of the future work, but one jest is of historic interest. Some thirty years ago I paid my first visit to Sanibel-Captiva in Florida, my favourite islands next to São Tomé e Príncipe. A nice lady showed me the local marine life, including their pride and joy, some basking manatees, cousins of the rarer dugong or sea cow. Dugongs live a solitary life of monogamous fidelity, which explains why they are rarer than manatees, who are almost as sex-crazed as dolphins and sea urchins. In spite of this, manatees are a threatened species, and suffer greatly from reckless boaters and fishers. The nice lady explained all this, and I instantly advised her to select her cutest manatee and call him Hugh. She asked why. "Then if anyone harmed him it would be a crime against Hugh Manatee." MGHIR! (this acronym for my solitary roaring will save time in the future) but she moved swiftly in the direction of away.

Since that jest Hugh Manatee has become a children's character and the name of a progressive rock fusion band based in Denver. Another of mine is the now-popular cocktail Tequila Mockingbird. I invented this in my first novel <u>The Speculator,</u> with a recipe. The novel was never published in print but an early e-publisher did so online. I was told once that everything that has appeared online lives for ever in some electronic Purgatory and can be retrieved from it, but I am now certain this is a myth. Tragically (for me) I lost my sole copy of the typescript, I suspect during a rapid move to escape a bookmaker. I know that it could not have been stolen. Burglars once broke into my apartment in Hollywood. They not only left my screenplay behind but gave me extensive notes. Many were helpful, although I never went with their main suggestion of making Beppo the Wonder Dog catch rabies and bite all the other characters in turn.

A dusty typescript of <u>The Speculator</u> may still exist somewhere in the back office of one of the agents who abandoned the task of representing it: "feel it would be fruitless to submit it to any more publishers... never known such a hostile environment in publishing ... do not trouble to send second novel... sadly feel unable to commit fully to your interests at this moment in time... pressure of work from established clients... etc etc". If miraculously it shows up I am glad to pay the return postage to Rubato Towers.

The screenplay version is still very much available, but amid the global depression I suspect nobody will need a guaranteed tax loss for a very long time.

<u>17 April</u>

A busy session working on my autobiography <u>My Goodness How I Roared!</u> I started to compile a list of my very best jests, to which I added an array of quips, bon mots and apophthegms from casual conversation. I compiled a separate list of famous people who had known me. I was gratified that each list quickly mounted to 25 closely-printed pages, and all before I had reached the age of 8.

This gave me an idea so inspired for monetizing my memoirs that I was compelled to do three hours frenetic housework to calm down. The wooden floor at Rubato Towers acquired such a sheen that the Resident Mouse used it with his chums for a skating competition, which was won by the neighbours' gerbil with a camel spin followed by a mule kick and a spectacular triple Axl Rose.

I thought: since I have so many famous people to spare and so much sparkling dialogue, why not auction a mention in my memoirs?

I will publish the full list of famous people who will appear in the index (memo to self: I will need a top-notch indexer and there may have to be an index to the index.) Then I will invite sealed bids for an appearance in the scene in which each one meets me. For an additional fee, I will give successful bidders a share in the dialogue, starting with a mumbled bon mot and ascending through quips, wisecracks and zingers to one of my very best jests. For the maximum fee, the jest will be greeted with collective hilarity. If too many bidders take up this offer I will have to abandon MGHIR! and use my alternative title: <u>Over Five Million Copies Sold!</u> I will allow people to bid for more than one famous person but with an upper limit of five, partly to secure financial fair play but also to stop people wondering why, at so many interesting encounters in my life I was accompanied by someone, as it might be Prodnose, who is otherwise completely ignored.

18 April

Of course there are many more serious victims of the crisis, but I cannot help thinking of the convenors of literary salons. These depend heavily on intimate, whispered bitchy confidences ("They say she took advantage of a special deal and had both of her faces lifted for the price of one") and therefore cannot be conducted by Zoom or whatever the thing's called. Social distancing has been ruinous for New York wits: if they gathered now at the Algonquin Round Table the blasted thing would have to be as big as a cricket pitch.

I have decided to begin my autobiography <u>My Goodness, How I Roared!</u> with the letter X. No one has ever done this before in the English language (it's too easy in Albanian, where they have had to introduce a new form of Scrabble to deal with the proliferation of Xs, Zs, and Qs.) It will give MGHIR!

a little extra life as a quiz night answer: which major work in English by a Nobel laureate begins with the letter X?

The composition of this opening sentence required extreme concentration. I closed the skating rink for the Resident Mouse and his chums and bribed them to picnic in the East Wing of Rubato Towers with the last of the Stilton. It leaves me with but a wedge of immature Cheddar (it mouths at me non-stop from the cheese board "Who are you looking at? Don't think I'm hard enough? Come here with that knife and you'll find out") but we must all make sacrifices for our art.

My first effort was "Xenophon was the first garter snake I ever loved." [Cliché button locks. Cue long passage of lonely, sensitive child having magic adventures with his little reptilian friend.] Reject. Moreover, it would be unfair to begin with an X in a proper name.

My second effort was more promising. "Xebecs bobbed at their anchors, their sails turning red in the sunset: that was my first view of the sleepy harbour of Kif-sur-Demande which was to be my home." [Cliché button locks again. Cue long passage of louche misadventures as a remittance man.] Reject, but store as a chapter title "Nothing Too Louche."

More toil, and a failed passage about my lifelong battle against Xerasia (dry hair). Finally I hit on: "Xylophones in the distance played an eerie spectral rhumba." Some ninety minutes later I deleted "eerie": if the rhumba was spectral, then "eerie" was supererogatory.

Prodnose: The day gone, and you have barely finished one sentence.

Myself (flicking imaginary speck of dust from faultless cuffs): That was how Madame Bovary was written and all of us since then have been grateful to Gussie Flaubert for showing us the way. I suppose you just crank your stuff out, like Tuppy

Trollope, five thousand words, anything will do, then off to the day job running the Post Office, or in your case, collecting the used rubber bands.

19 April

I am grateful for all the xenia (small gifts) from my public, suggesting alternative ways of beginning my autobiography <u>My Goodness How I Roared!</u> with the letter X. But I am sticking to my original idea, since xylophones at twilight will always remind me of my beloved São Tomé e Príncipe. I have made a few amendments for reasons which will be clear to anyone who had to learn to touch-type on an old manual typewriter. (Yes, child, can you believe it? We had to press a separate lever for each letter, and a little bell would ring and we had to retract by hand something called the carriage.)

The new opening will be "Xylophones hammered out a funky jazz quickstep to the crows in the waving baobabs."

A new sentence of this kind is clearly needed in Rubato Towers, where after fornicating all night the brown fox is no longer quick and could not jump over a lazy daisy let alone a dog of any size. (Note to self: store Lazy Daisy as name of new children's character, who becomes a hero during lockdown.)

Curses! The telephone. It showed an unknown American number. I answered and it proved to be Joe Biden. He asked me to write his campaign autobiography. "I am honoured, Mr Vice-President, but you must call it My Time." Why, he obligingly asked. "Then the cover could be printed as BIDEN MY TIME." He is renowned for his sunny temperament, but he gave no response and so this was another case of MGHIR! I rushed to the piano to give him another piece of advice. "For your campaign song, you must use the bouncy number by Harold Arlen and Yip Harburg: Happiness Is A Thing Called Joe." I played him a few bars, and do you know, he hung up.

Ah well. At least he has become another famous name to put into my auction. I expect a high bid for him, especially if as now seems happily likely he replaces T Ronald Dump.

20 April

Confirming that housework is more violent exercise than cricket, I strained my back mopping the ground floor at Rubato Towers. I blame the communal mop, which is the wrong size for me. After just a few swabs I felt as if I had batted for 20 overs (a rare experience, I admit) with a child's bat. But thanks to this interfering government, I cannot now go to the mop-makers in Savile Row to have one hand tailored.

The back pain made me want a real drink for the first time in lockdown. Like many solitary artists before me, I make a point of never taking one alone, since one readily becomes three or even seven, but until now I had never thought of relaxing my rule so as to drink in company by video call. It seems to be all the rage. I telephoned a likely acquaintance and when his image appeared I enjoyed a delightful conversation lubricated by bracing tots from my special supply of Glenmiller Very Special Single Malt whisky ("it's s-m-o-o-t-h"), all the more delightful because I didn't have to offer him a drop. Heh-heh.

Video drinking at home may well take hold after the crisis is over and it will be a serious threat to our surviving pubs when they re-open. You choose your drinking companions – no risk of the self-opiniated loudmouth who hangs around the bar foisting himself on you. (It occurs to me that America for the last four years has been like a tiny saloon where no one can escape the yammering voice of T Ronald Dump.) No pressure to get your round in, and remembering what every person wanted, worrying whether they will accept substitutes and seeing the barperson's surprise and resentment when you ask for a tray. No wondering when or if your tightwad friend will get his round in, and whether he will try to pay for it again with that dusty white five-pound note which they have never seen before. No overpriced bar snacks you would never think of eating anywhere else. No ambient television with hysterical commentary on the national paintdrying championships when you want to watch the cricket. No ambient jukebox playing some twerp's selections, no ambient hellish video games. Easy access to a lavatory. No overcrowded car park or a desperate search for space in some dim, dangerous back street. And of course no risk of being thrown out.

After the seventh agreeable back-numbing Glenmiller I took a policy decision to become insensible on the settee and postponed further work on my autobiography.

<u>21 April</u>

Her Majesty's real birthday. So sad that I will not be able to go to her party this year and play her usual favourites from the Doors on the piano. Would offer to do this virtually from Rubato Towers, but the wretched thing remains out of tune and the Royal ear is acute.

I woke up on the settee with a throbbing head.

Prodnose: You have a settee with a throbbing head? (Cackles).

Myself (indulgently): He has a very limited life and one allows him a few moments. To be more precise: Still on the settee, I awoke in a cramped diagonal with a throbbing head, a dry mouth, a sore throat, and a flush hotter than the one I drew in New Orleans against Edward G Robinson all those years ago. I had a moment's alarm. Could this be COVID or its poor relation, Mandelson? But then I saw the remains of the Glenmiller bottle and realized I was in familiar territory. I stumbled to the emergency cabinet and reached for the prewar Fernet Branca I laid down for moments like these. It was the work of moments to mix it with equal parts lime juice, ginger ale and Menorcan gin (Xoriguer of course, for alphabetical reasons) and after a deep draught I was able to complete the "daily dozen", the exercise régime I devised before I discovered housework.

I felt strong enough to return to my autobiography
My Goodness How I Roared! But the first two
words "Xylophones hammered..." were enough to
revive the throbbing headache.

I reached for one of my discards: "'Xysti were such
an elegant feature of Greek villas in this period,'
said the suave estate agent, Mr Feta Kompli,
indicating the handsome long covered portico for
athletic exercises or general recreation and
conversation." Memories... Memories... [punches
cliché button] flooded back. Quite. Memories never
trickle or even gush. They flood. As so often with
estate agents, Mr Kompli's tactics succeeded. I fell
in love with the best feature of the villa and signed
the lease, overlooking the flaky plaster, the
mildewed kitchen, the singing lavatory and the
largely absent roof. I spent most of my first months
in Taramasalata in that confounded xystum,
cursing the Durrells who had induced me to go
there. Eventually I took a poky room above the

Café Eczorbatance and painstakingly completed my first novel <u>Stoned Olives.</u>[28]

---

[28] Stoned Olives later become The Speculator.

A rare roar from Prodnose

22 April

Too many people know that I attended Repton School in my giddy youth for me to deny it. Other famous writers who went there include Christopher Isherwood and his chum Edward Upward, who lived to be 105 and might have been a relative of the more gifted Luke, Vernon Watkins, Roald Dahl, who left a savage portrait of his headmaster Geoffrey Fisher, the future Archbishop of Canterbury, the now fashionable Denton Welch, and James Fenton who was up at the same time as me and with whom I once acted on the musical stage.

Prodnose: Get on with it!

Myself (to myself): He has become insufferable since his little moment yesterday.

The Resident Mouse: Get on with it!

Myself: Et tu, brute? (Sings) "Tute frute, o rute! Tute frute, o rute! Tute frute, o rute! Tute frute et tu brute? Nunc pro tunc quoque quam amabam!" (A beat. MGHIR! again). It was Repton that taught me enough Latin to cover this great song as Ricardus Parvus but not enough to become a judge by passing the rigorous judging exam…

The Fornicating Foxes: Get on with it!

Myself: It is futile to swim against a riptide of small minds. At Repton for breakfast we were often served toast with scrambled powdered egg. I think it was left over from the war which we had won over fifteen years previously. I grew quite fond of it, as of my genuine fake Rolex watch I bought in Macao (closes eyes) ah Macao in the old days when it was still Portuguese, a beautiful backwater where time itself always had time on its hands , when I spent nights on the tiles playing mah jongg with ancient General Fan-tan drinking his bitter tea and waiting for him to drop a clue to the location of the fabled lost city of Kashankari...

Prodnose, Mouse, Foxes: Get on with it!

Myself (opening eyes, I hope in a marked manner): I learnt to enjoy powdered egg once I had learnt to stop expecting it to be anything like the real thing.

At the start of the crisis I laid in a stock of the stuff before I knew that Britain's hens would go into patriotic overdrive and fill supermarkets as usual, and was finally tempted to try it. I followed the instructions but it was nothing like Repton's finest. Even with frantic top-ups of the powder I obtained only a grisly gruel, which was rejected indignantly by the Resident Mouse. I have written to Dame Vera Lynn for advice, since she remembers how we won the war, and have offered in exchange to accompany her next comeback tour.[29]

---

[29] Dame Vera, the wartime Forces' Sweetheart, was then 103.

23 April

Four more tigers and three lions have come down with the virus at the Bronx Zoo and there has been no update on Nadia. I fear that she has perished. This would be a fatal blow to the plummeting poll ratings of T Ronald Dump, and I am certain that he has ordered its concealment. Any Nadia who appears at the Zoo will be an impostrix. They should check whether she has three missing vibrissae on her right side and ask her the name of her first dental hygienist.

A new effort to use the powdered egg produced a pallid, putrid paste. I took it outdoors and left it as revenge on the foxes. There were especially eldritch screeches last night: I suspect that the foxes were dogging. I await the eggy advice of Dame Vera Lynn, who apart from her wonderful singing helped the war effort with a recipe book titled Whale Meat Again. I know that she used powdered egg in her instructions for White Sauce with Dover Sole, to which she added the surprising recommendation "serve with Bluebird Liquorice Toffee if you can get it."[30]

In spite of the powdered egg failure I felt strong enough to resume my autobiography <u>My Goodness, How I Roared!</u> I tried out a new opening: "Xcalak at last! I told my faithful mahout I would walk the rest of the way and slipped off my faithful elephant, giving her the last of my breath mints as a parting gift before accepting her farewell kiss. I gazed at the ... Mexican village [punches cliché button] sleepy Mexican village in the southern province of Quintana Rooney, by the ... bay [punches cliché button] azure bay in whose clear waters I hoped to film the rare mating dance of the golden xiphias..." Yes, I know that Xcalak is a proper name, but it deserves to be better known. I never sighted the golden xiphias but I did return to Xcalak to use it as the location for <u>The Adequate Six,</u> my low-budget remake of <u>The Magnificent</u>

---

[30] Vera Lynn's major wartime songs were "We'll Meet Again" and "(There'll Be Bluebirds Over) The White Cliffs Of Dover." Bluebird Liquorice Toffee is a traditional British candy.

Seven. Ah, the hack jobs I had to accept before I became famous.

After several hours' furious pacing I went back to my first choice opening. But I had hardly set down "Xylophones hammered…" when the telephone rang. It was the Dalai Lama. It knew it was him because the normal boring ring tone was replaced by a deep gong. Before he could speak I sang "Well, hello Dalai!" He is an even bigger giggler than Joe Biden but there was a frost from the other end you could have bottled in the Himalayas, so once again it was a case of MGHIR! Perhaps he had heard it before.

The Dalai Lama was anxious to know if he would be appearing in my autobiography. "Well, of course you are, my dear old holy thing!" I did not tell him that I expected to get a good bid for an appearance with him. But even without my proposed auction, I could hardly avoid mentioning his great kindness in substituting for me at the last minute when I was unable to open and bless the newly-built Test cricket stadium at Dharamshala. When the Obamas finally let me go, I joined him there and we had a very good net,[31] although he never quite got the hang of overarm bowling.

<u>24 April</u>

Browsing through my <u>Guide To Unstarred Movies</u> ("If you get a chance, miss them") I was surprised to discover even cheaper re-makes of <u>The Magnificent Seven</u>. There was an English version called <u>The Not-Really-Famous Five</u>, a version with some superannuated action stars called <u>The Flab Four,</u> and one, I think meant as a parody, <u>The Dead Soppy Three.</u> The score for that one was credited to Mal Loesser, the jealous brother of Frank, and subject of his abandoned musical project <u>The Most Unhappy Fella.</u> Not only a mediocre composer, Mal was also a nasty piece of work, once described at the fabled Algonquin Elliptical Table (the one used when the Round one had to be cleaned) as "the evil of two Loessers." I play a lot of Frank Loesser for the neighbours, but it often comes out like Mal.

---

[31] Cricket practice in an enclosed space similar to a batting cage at baseball.

Joy! I learnt how to cook the powdered egg. Vera Lynn kindly came through for me. What a trouper! She advised me to add powdered milk. She added: "Tastes even better with powdered water if you can get it." She's always been a bit of a wag, as I discovered when researching the notes for my musical tribute to Al Bowlly[32] which the neighbours so much enjoyed on its try-out performance. (It later broke all records in Footscray.)

My powdered egg took me right back to school. There is nothing else I like to remember about the food except the wonderful Bakewell tart which would occasionally appear from a cook who came from Bakewell. More usually the pudding was something hideous in the sago family. I have a recurring nightmare that I am back at school lunch facing a plate of sago. The Boy Who Actually Liked Sago and would actually eat everyone else's is missing and I have to finish the thing myself. That one always makes me wake up in a... a... [punches cliché button] ... a cold sweat.

---

[32] 1930s British crooner, who outperformed Bing Crosby.

My housemaster regularly said the graces at meals in the wrong order. "For what we have received..." at the beginning, "for what we are about to receive" at the end. I used to think this was absence of mind (when helping me to complete a university entrance form he asked "What's your first name, Richard?", years before "Don't tell him, Pike.") But I now realize he might have intended an ironic comment on the food: thanking the Lord for all the meals we had ever eaten before and all the meals we were going to eat afterwards, but not the actual one we faced on our plates.

It was delightful to chat yesterday to my old chum the Dalai Lama, but I could not help thinking of the brutal wretch who now controls his country and will choose his eventual successor. Mr Xi is a disgrace to the letter X and from now on I shall use the old Wade-Giles transliteration and call him Mr Hsi. Thinking of him and the highly-placed people in our country who kowtow to him brought on my of my "funny turns". I smashed more of the non-visitor crockery in Rubato Towers, frightened the Resident Mouse, and lost another day of progress on my autobiography <u>My Goodness How I Roared!</u>

<u>25 April</u>

I have had many chats with the dear old Dalai Lama but not with his vice-captain Gedhun Choekyi Nyima, the Panchen Lama. This is mainly because he was taken into "protective custody" by the Chinese in 1995 and has not been seen since. I could not even wish him a happy 31st birthday today.

I have been in touch with the designer and maker of the Trump baby balloon to see what they would charge for executing a similar model of the Paramount Brute now ruling China. They can't be too busy right now and should offer a reasonable rate. I shall invite Jeremy Corbyn to its launch after lockdown, with all the other Celebrities who demonstrated with the Trump baby balloon. I am certain they will accept: they would not wish to show a selective conscience. If the blimp-makers offer a 2 for 1 deal I would like my Baby Hsi (see yesterday re spelling) to be accompanied by one of his highly-placed helpers in this country but I am spoilt for choice. Perhaps they could do a coronablimp instead.

Lockdown conditions are producing a comeback by nature in other locations besides Rubato Towers. A report comes in of a giant jellyfish described as a giant stinger basking in a canal in Venice. This seems most implausible. I think this might have been a misprint for stinker and the sighting was of Sir Philip Green.[33]

26 April

It wasn't Sir Philip Green but a real jellyfish. I mean, the strange object they saw basking in a Venetian canal. Apparently they used to be as common there as plastic is now. It must have been

---

[33] British billionaire businessman, feted by Tony Blair as retail genius and knighted, later widely condemned for extravagance, tax avoidance, and unfairness towards pensioners of his failed business, British Home Stores.

a bit tough for the Doge of Venice in its serenest days. There you are, lying back in your gondola enjoying the last Cornetto, and you absent-mindedly trail your other hand in the water and ah-merda! you've been stung and the gondolier has to drop everything and urinate on it to take the pain away and all the Venetian plebs start sniggering and saying that's what they've always wanted to do and can they get in the queue…

It is a very serious matter if jellyfish are making a comeback in Venice, or anywhere else, because they are sex-crazed. Forget foxes. Forget dolphins. Forget even the sea urchin. Jellyfish: sex, sex, sex, that's all they've got on the brain. Not that they have much of a brain, but all it has room for is sex. When they're not having sex, all they do is watch plankton porn. Nothing very romantic about jellyfish sex. Wham, bam, never mind thank you, sting each other, urinate over each other (a gentleman jellyfish always goes first) and then they are at it again. I wrote all this up, in more scientific language, for my favourite publication, the Journal of Molluscan Studies, only to have it rejected on the pedantic grounds that jellyfish are not molluscs. They are, as a matter of fact, fish. A collection of them, as in a murder of crows, is technically a smack although a more frequently used expression is an aws**t of jellyfish.

Even before the virus cleaned up the seas for them, jellyfish were proliferating because they have only one natural predator, the sea turtle. And while jellyfish are sex-crazed, sea turtles are definitely not. They can hardly be bothered to breed, and many are gay although they have not dared yet to swim out of the closet. Unlike gay giraffes, who have come a long way since poor Victor. They stage their own Pride marches in rainbow-coloured spots and you can see them necking openly in their own bars and clubs.

Without sea turtles, the only way to eliminate jellyfish is to open more sushi bars. (Sings) If you knew sushi, like I know sushi… (Pauses. Once again, MGHIR!) They serve jellyfish. I once had the taster menu in a sushi bar (in Xochimilcho, rhymes with Bilko, on my way back from Xcalak, since you ask.) Jellyfish. Sea urchin. Sea cucumber. All the things I hate to see snorkelling offered to me on a plate. I blunted the agony with agave.

27 April

Boris Johnson has been returned to Downing Street like a parcel. Did a neighbour sign for him?

Prodnose: I thought you were laying off him?

Myself: Resumption of my normal insult service will tell him that he is fully recovered. (To myself) Gnat-brained dullard who needed water wings in the gene pool.

I notice from pictures a problem for our leader. Because of social distancing regulations, he is no longer able to have his hair hand-tousled by his usual salonist and he is clearly doing the job for himself.

Even in periods of penury I have never stinted on a good haircut, and the same expert hands have tended my hair through thin and thin for the last thirty years. This policy has stood me in good stead (questions to myself: does stead exist except to be stood in, and can it be bad as well as good?) during lockdown: my hair retains its shape and if Boris Johnson sets us all free today I could go out to meet my public without a qualm.

On my last visit to the salon they tried to sell me some special shampoo. When they told me the price of a vial, I exclaimed "That's over 10p a hair!" and for once there was roaring in the plural.

I hear that President T Ronald Dump tested his bleach virus remedy on his hair. It worked perfectly there but unfortunately some leaked into his brain. Dump's poll ratings continue to plummet. I advised my friend Rory Bremner to take care of the Pence in his famous impressions, but the man of so many voices was notably silent and once again MGHIR!

President Dump now claims that he was being sarcastic. As Commander-in-chief he should know better than to use sarcasm. The armed forces are trained to interpret orders literally and to execute them at once. One recalls the alarm years ago when Ronald Reagan said into a live microphone that he had ordered the bombing of Russia. Reagan was a trained actor but even he experienced difficulty in conveying that this was a joke. Dump has acted only in the theatre of his own ego, the script written by himself, directed by himself, to bouquets thrown by himself. This entire Presidency is like a modern version of the entertainment proposed by Toad on his return to Toad Hall, until quashed by Badger.

TWEET. . . . BY TOAD.
(There will be other tweets by TOAD during the evening.)
ADDRESS. . . BY TOAD
SYNOPSIS — My medical genius… my Noble prize nominations… Golf and how to play it… Beating the lame…
SONG. . . . BY TOAD. (Composed by himself.)
OTHER COMPOSITIONS. BY TOAD
will be sung in the course of the evening by the. . . COMPOSER.

Prodnose: You've added nothing to your autobiography for days.

Myself: I'm waiting for you to make me a decent cup of tea, That's all it took for Marcel bloody Proust, or Marjeli Proops[34] as he called himself in his Agony Auntie column for the Almanach de Gotha[35]. (To myself). His tea leaves much to be desired and his coffee gives grounds for imprisonment.

29 April

Thinking reluctantly about Mike Pence put me in mind of the last Indiana Vice-President, Dan Quayle. Although never an intimate, he got to know me quite well during his four years of celebrity.

---

[34] Marjorie Proops was the long-serving advice columnist for Britain's Daily Mirror.
[35] A directory of Europe's royalty and higher nobility.

As a special correspondent, I covered his Vice-Presidential campaign in 1988. This was a fascinating experience, not for the candidate but for the locations. Quayle had made a number of "gaffes" on the stump (a gaffe is any occurrence in a political campaign in which a candidate reveals his or her real self) and he had been famously mauled in the TV debate by his courtly Texan rival, Lloyd Bentsen. Quayle was therefore being hidden in safely Republican townships in safe Red states (American political colorings are the reverse of British: Red is Right, Blue a little less Right.) Through the Quayle campaign I therefore found a public in states which I had never visited before. I finished on the university campus in Stillwater, Oklahoma. They asked me to give an address but I thought this would be unfair on the candidate and I had to file my report on him. I would be glad to return to Stillwater, should they still be pining.

By gum, it was hard to get a story from the Quayle campaign. The same motorcade, the same stump speech with the same admiring reference to the high school football team. I have seen dozens of politicians attempt the same stunt in dozens of countries. Why do they imagine voters will be impressed with a ritual invocation prepared by the lowest drudge on their staff? There is no good reason for any important visitor to know about the local school team. The only politician who could get away with that sort of thing was Bill Clinton, who had almost extra-terrestrial powers of empathy with any and every member of any audience of any size. I believe that was due to his early training in Arkansas politics, where one is expected to master the personal details of every significant voter in each of its (as I remember) 75 counties. No problem at all for a card-index memory like Clinton's and when I saw him in his home state four years later, it was all "Hi there, Billy-Bob, still raising that hog?" or "Howdy, Alice, still baking that angel food cake?" (My apologies if it was Alice who raised the hog and Billy-Bob who baked the angel food cake.)

During the first Bush Presidency I was visiting Washington DC and the now Vice-President asked me for an interview. I had a little time on my hands after reorganizing the Smithsonian so I agreed. I gave instructions to reception at the Hay-Adams to admit him to my suite, and had just rejected room service's first selection of Oreos, when Quayle asked me to the office he had been assigned in the White House. This was not nearly so convenient, but I picked my way over the brooms and janitor's supplies and found a box where I could sit and record what I said to him. Quayle belied his reputation and displayed symptoms of coherence: he needed far less of my material than many other Celebrities.

As a parting gift I gave him one of my best lines. He was facing a difficult audience of critics of some pet wheeze of the Bush administration. My line was intended as a casual, witty dismissal of their carping pessimism. Unfortunately he delivered it with plodding solemnity, and it went into the annals of dumb Quaylisms. Anyway, here it is: "If we don't succeed, we run the risk of failure."

Quayle gave a much more gracious concession to Bill Clinton on election night 1992 than the senior

Bush, who was clearly peeved. This was surprising, because the elder Bush was renowned for his good manners and was idolized by his Secret Service detail, as one of them naughtily revealed to me on a campaign stop.

For some years Quayle sent me a Christmas card with an image of him and his family blessing me and mine. This stopped after I sent him one of my books.

<u>30 April</u>

Production of new cricket bats has been hit very hard by the lockdown, and one is astonished that the government has not designated this an essential industry. Very intricate process making a decent bat. At one stage the surface has to be rubbed repeatedly to lubricate it with natural oil from a horse's shin. It must be very tricky to get the horse to stand still for long enough, unless of course it is one of those I back at the races. I realize too late that I should have been betting at dressage events instead, where horses have to create the illusion of motion in one place.

Prodnose: So how's the autobiography? Have those xylophones finished hammering? (Chortles).

Myself: I am not producing McProse, such as yours, flipping familiar phrases into an 800-word burger. A once-in-a-lifetime banquet such as my autobiography requires immense preparation: assembly of the freshest figures of speech, getting to the market at opening time for the arrival of the first catch of synecdoche and the early season zeugma, their combination into a unique palette of…

Prodnose: Sounds more like Gourmet Night at Fawlty Towers.[36] (Guffaws)

---

[36] An especially brilliant episode of the British TV sitcom of the 1970s set in a resort hotel run by an incompetent martinet (Basil, played by John Cleese). Basil plans to attract a better class of clientele with a gourmet night but it founders in a series of calamities.

Myself (to myself): If one saw him on a plate of sushi, one would suddenly warm to the adjacent sea cucumber, sea urchin and jellyfish. But the wretch has a point. MGHIR! has suffered in the hurly-burly of lockdown life at Rubato Towers.

(Much later). "Xylophones hammered out a funky jazz quickstep to the crows in the waving baobabs. Ylang-ylang suffused the bath water, my choice from the luxurious natural oils on offer from the aspirational resort management. Zephyrs wafted through the open window additional notes of coco, peri-peri, thymesup, muskelon, amberrudd and patchouliclark. I lay back and breathed a heady cocktail of Sãotomean air." There. Undoubtedly the world's first major literary work to begin not only with an X but also a subsequent Y and Z.

The time and effort required to compose this are something the world's Prodnoses will never understand. Unable to scour the shops for salsify, I supped on one of my store cupboard recipes. Tuna on tuna. Open a can of tuna. Drain contents and put them on a plate. Open another can of tuna. Repeat. Serve with tuna. Tuna, tuna everywhere, but can I get one for the piano? MGHIR!

1 May (Maypoles banned as breach of social distancing)

No one seems to know why bat shit became the acme of craziness. It seems very unfair. Like all creatures bats have to shit sometimes, and they often have to wait until all the bears have left the woods. There was a wonderful nature film about bats some years ago, and the star was Mama Bat. She flits around all night. Partying? No way. Desperately looking for food for Baby Bat. Finally she does a supermarket swoop on something and schleps it home – a bat cave with thousands of baby bats, all kicking off for food at a pitch beyond even my reach at the piano at Rubato Towers. In all that kickoffony, Mama Bat can tell which individual squawk belongs to her baby. What a performer! She should take over from the pelican as the emblem of motherhood. No mention of any help from Papa Bat. Probably does not even shave, like Daddy

Pig,[37] and just hangs upside down in the cave watching sports replays. Maybe some mama bats can't take it any more, and they're the ones that go crazy.

However, it would take ten thousand overwrought mama bats dumping in the same place at once to generate the President of the United States.

I am not thinking of his "Let them drink bleach" moment (channelling the spirit of Marie-Antoinehairnette): after all, that became retrospective sarcasm. I refer to his theory that the Chinese encouraged the spread of coronavirus to help Joe Biden become President. This is monomania. Frank Sinatra used to perform a song called "Everything Happens To Me." It is not a favorite of the neighbours at Rubato Towers, but I made a special recording of it for Donald Trump to use as his campaign song to reflect his world view. Anything bad can be fitted into this message. The

---

[37] Father of the popular children's character Peppa Pig and generally shown as an incompetent

United States is still fighting to eradicate the boll weevil, the flying pest which eats its cotton crops. (Actually, there are two varieties: the giant boll weevil and the lesser of two weevils.) Watch out for Trump to claim that the Chinese and the Iranians have engineered a new strain (in a new axis of weevil) to attack him, but he's ordered a new wall in the sky.

Trump's condition has prompted much talk of the 25th Amendment. Unfortunately, this is very badly drafted, as I warned them at the time. It is based on a Catch similar to that invented by my namesake Joseph. (In a delightful conversation years ago, we established that he was not related to me.) Anyway, Catch-25 requires the President to certify himself bat-shit crazy, but if he is capable of doing this then he cannot be crazy. Alternatively, Vice-President Farthing[38] and eight Cabinet members can certify that he is indeed bat-shit crazy, but if Trump denies it we get a long scene familiar to watchers of pantomime: oh yes, you are... oh no, I'm not... oh

---

[38] A pretty little English coin, worth one quarter of an old penny (plural pence), phased out in 1956.

yes, you are... oh no, I'm not. That would take the United States to the so far unused 26th amendment provision in which the live audience is asked to shout for one side or the other[39]. I fear that Trump supporters would win this contest. Indeed, Trump could win it on his own.

Prodnose: Not getting very far in your autobiography today. Are the zephyrs still wafting? (Cackles).

Myself (Continuing to polish a silver bibelot with a retired pair of Old Reptonian spats): The scene on election night when Trump blames me for his overthrow should provide a satisfying final chapter.

---

[39] British pantomime is a traditional and still popular entertainment in which an old story such as Cinderella is retold with corny jokes, slapstick comedy and songs. It has strict conventions, including gender reversal (hero played by female actor, comic woman by a man) and a scene resolved by two halves of an audience shouting against each other.

2 May

Back to my autobiography. "I ylay-ylay ylanguidly for the ylast time in the ylang-ylang infused bathwater. Then I arose with a mighty yleap. It was time for the first of the great experiments I performed in São Tomé e Príncipe which caused such jealousy when I reported them to the Royal Society. I stepped out onto the veranda and allowed the warm wafting zephyrs to dry my body au naturel. Astonished nightingales lifted their heads and made such a racket you could have heard them in Berkeley Square. I stepped back into the bathroom and observed that the bathwater had settled into a flat calm. Now for my experiment.

"As any fule no, even Prodnose, in laboratory conditions bathwater spins clockwise through a plughole in the northern hemisphere, and anti-clockwise in the southern due to the Coriolanus effect. But what would it do precisely on the Equator? The grateful resort management had given me the prize suite, where the line exactly bisected the bath. With a deft flick of the wrist, perfected by years of bowling the zombie, the zamboni, the zooter, the zorker (continues page 947), I pulled the plug. The result was as I had predicted. The bathwater remained perfectly still. It simply had no idea which way to spin. I had to swirl it myself to remove it. I confirmed my result over the next two days by borrowing the baths on either side. The northern bathwater span, painfully slowly, clockwise, the southern, equally slowly, counterclockwise.

"Later, walking precisely along the line of the Equator, I found some baffled spiders who had no idea which way to begin spinning their webs.

"The next morning I went to the achingly beautiful Praia Café beach, also bisected by the line, with a new cricket ball. They had never seen such an object in São Tomé e Príncipe and the airport customs officer actually asked if it was an offensive weapon. 'Not the way I bowl it,' I replied in a flash. Lost of course on him: MGHIR! In those days I was a swing bowler who could move the ball both ways off the bat. I found the Equator line on the beach and took one pace to the north. I bowled my customary outswinger.⁴⁰ I picked up the ball and crossed the Equator, one pace to the south. With no change of grip or action I bowled my first delivery in the southern hemisphere. And it reversed! In the contrary southern airflow the ball acquired a new character of swing. I went back to the resort, bought a celebratory jug of margaritas to share with the other residents, then slipped into the pool to begin my second novel <u>Swimming To Infinity</u>."

3 May

I am ending my autobiography MGHIR! at the point where Donald Trump blames me for his overthrow, but I cannot decide which version to use. The one where he screams my name in impotent rage or the one where he is a blubbering hulk, pleading for forgiveness. Perhaps both. I am not proposing to pronounce to him "You're fired", a scene which would reach Force 9 on the Prodnose Scale of Triteness.

---

[40] Similar to a curve ball which breaks away from a right-handed batter

When I complete MGHIR! in this way, I hope that I may finally be allowed to retire from the rostrums I occupy in official life. I shall go first to Pakistan, to say a long farewell to my friends and public there but also to purchase a lime plantation and establish a cricket ground and facilities with it. If pressed, I shall inaugurate this with my repertoire of zombies, zambonis, zooters, zorkers (continues page 9471 et seq). I wonder if Younus Khan would care to receive them? It is especially satisfying to deliver to a fellow artist. Pakistani limes, like their mangoes, are uniquely wonderful and their juice does not even need tequila and Triple Sec, but there are several varieties and I shall have to organize a blind tasting programme: What's My Lime?[41]

When I have made my choice, I shall introduce the variety to my beloved São Tomé e Príncipe, where I have already been allotted one of their spare islands. Even with the cares of a lime plantation, I might succumb to the country's particular version of langour, called léve-léve (although couchez-

---

[41] A long-running BBC television quiz of the 1950s, modelled on "The Name's The Same," on which my aunt Joan was a regular star panellist.

couchez might be more appropriate), so I will repeat my offer to become Her Britannic Majesty's representative to the country. However, I shall report only to HBM in person, knowing her wicked sense of humour at the Scrabble board. I really do not wish to submit anything through the present Foreign Secretary, Mr Draab. My first priority will be to get the International Cricket Council to relocate from boring old Dubai (there's no there, there, as dear old Gertrude Stein once said about somewhere else). São Tomé e Príncipe is perfect for the headquarters of world cricket, since, as I established yesterday, you can play a match in both hemispheres at the same time. Especially if I am bowling.

4 May

To occupy myself further in my impending retirement, I have offered to become the correspondent in São Tomé e Príncipe for the world-renowned Journal of Molluscan Studies. I have just enjoyed its incisive piece on "The complete mitochondrial genomes from the endemic family Baicaliidae (Caenogastropodia: Truncatelloida)." If the Journal fails to snap me up, I hope to benefit from the intense circulation war in the mollusc world by making the same offer to its rival Molluscan Research.

In truth, I cannot remember many molluscs when snorkelling on my last visit to the islands, in either hemisphere. I saw countless specimens of a hand-sized silvery fish which I have never identified. With apologies for the anthropomorphism, it looked uncommonly as if it was wearing a shiny suit and flashing a perpetual smile, so I dubbed it the politician fish. I was depressed to read recently that São Tomé e Príncipe, whose waters teemed with fish, now imports frozen fish from China, confirming my view that any country which trades with Mr Hsi's China does so on terms set by Mr Hsi.

Prodnose: Why do you keep calling him Mr Hsi instead of Mr Xi?

Myself (with a snarl): I told you before. Don't ask me again or I shall stage a Hsi fit! (Pauses. MGHIR! again. To myself) I don't know why I bother with him. If Prodnose had been the Pope he would have commissioned Michelangelo to whitewash the Sistine Chapel.

I notice that Mr Hsi has been foisting his Thoughts on the Chinese people as Mao did before. I was told that some Western universities actually teach them. If that is so, I urge their alumni to convert their degrees, before they become tainted, to a respected degree in Hamburgerology from the McDonald University. (I did not make this up. Does Ronald hand them out on graduation day?)

Of course paramount dictators do many worse things but they have a terrifying power to publish their works and make people read them. When I visited Albania after the final fall of Communism the streets were clogged with those of Enver Hoxha. At least the dead despot left his people some means of heating their houses in winter. Mao should have had to send his stuff to publishers and agents like the rest of us and endured their rejection letters. I never fell below Level D, the terse postcard, but he might have attracted a Level Z (based on one sent in 1928 by an Australian publisher Angus & Robertson): "Dear Mr Tung, No, you may not send us your remaining Thoughts, and we will not give you the name of another publisher. We hate no rival publishers sufficiently to ask you to inflict them on them."

Modern dictators make one feel more kindly towards Nero, who expected his subjects only to cheer him at the chariot races and applaud his imitation of Francus Sinatrus, the popular contemporary balladeer celebrated for Mea Via.

5 May

I have decided to feel sorry for myself. After all, nobody else does. I know it is hard to believe but I do regular long lengths in an infinity pool of existential despair. For the sake of my public I have learnt to wear a mask under the mask. Now, on my rare outdoor forays for root vegetables, the government asks me to wear a mask over the mask over the mask.

I have not always been the genial boulevardier of Rubato Towers, the flannelled flaneur of the cricket field, the casual caresser of cocktail choruses on the calliope. I have waited long hours at Destiny station only to find that my train has left from another platform. I have taken a bulging suitcase of troubles down to Madame Rue[42]. I have stared at Lonely Street from my dormer window in Heartbreak Hotel. I have ordered the Blue Plate Special at the Sad Café.

The Resident Mouse: You think you've got it bad? I came here to sell the Big Issue.

---

[42] Discovered I've been performing this wrongly for over fifty years. Love Potion Number Nine, covered in UK by the Searchers, actually refers to Madame Ruth and her gold-capped tooth, and not Madame Rue with her bold tattoo.

Myself: The mountains of metaphor part once again to bring forth a ridiculous mouse.

All writers have known this condition. Even my model, Gussie Flaubert, had his moments of wanting to chuck in his novels. He nearly accepted an offer to come to England and work for one of the new Christmas card companies.

For me, the condition began with the discovery that every single literary agent, every single publisher, every single film studio, every single publication, even the worthy Journal of Molluscan Studies, is run by Prodnoses. What else explains their long silences at my submissions and the final grudging acknowledgement and rejection? Its main effect is a jereboam of jealousy towards every other published writer, even friends: why him, why her? (Gore Vidal, my regular host, admitted similar feelings in the sauna at Ravello.)

I know that the murmured appreciation of cognoscenti means more than the raucous cheers of a multitude of fools. But on days like these I wish that my fifty-year literary career had known just one moment of rauc. Woe, woe, woe, thrice woe. I am re-titling my autobiography <u>Nobody Roared.</u>

<u>6 May</u>

My heartfelt thanks to all my worldwide friends and public who roared for me yesterday. My special thanks to my neighbours who roared especially loudly and persistently at my evening recital at the keyboard in Rubato Towers (which has mysteriously recovered from its previous electronic malady). I gave them an extended edition of "Love Potion Number Nine", the song I inadvertently misquoted yesterday, and do you know, the neighbours roared for it over and over again? I still think that Madame Rue with a gold or bold tattoo is a better name for the central figure and I am certain that the lyricist, the great Jerry Leiber, would have agreed with me had I been able to suggest it to him. Unfortunately, I was only 10 at the time and had probably been kept in again after school for correcting the English teacher.

Sadly, I have missed other such opportunities and not only in song lyrics. Had I only been at NASA at the time, I could have spared Neil Armstrong the sappy line they gave him when he stepped on the Moon. No wonder he misquoted it. But that is another story.

Anyway, I was quite restored by yesterday's roars. All the black bile disappeared and the old heart pumped the milk of kindness by the quart through every vein. I gave the last of the Camembert to the Resident Mouse. Only the rules on social distancing stopped me from washing the feet of the local beggars.

At times like these we should all set ourselves to promote optimism and good feelings. During the Great Depression, the Mayor of New York, James J "Gentleman Jimmy" Walker (the most dapper incumbent and the last public figure of note to sport spats until I revived them for afternoon wear) asked all songwriters to compose only happy songs. Hizonner, himself the lyricist of a sugary ballad "Will You Love Me In December As You Do

In May?", was dead right. For the same reason, President Franklin D Roosevelt fêted Shirley Temple in the White House for her contribution to national revival. I am surprised that Boris Johnson, who runs coronavirus policy like an old edition of War Picture Library[43], has not revived the wartime regulations against spreading alarm and despondency. We all know that the virus has agents everywhere listening for stories of NHS shortages or rotten planning and it is our clear duty to keep these from him. Conversely, the virus is baffled by stories of British pluck and phlegm. "Himmel," he exclaims in his War Picture German, "zese British never know when zey are beaten!"

It is not only my patriotic duty to spread uplift but there is good money in it. I bet when Thomas Jefferson scribbled that phrase about the "pursuit of happiness" he never imagined he would spawn a

---

[43] A popular series of comics in 1950s Britain although they would now probably be called graphic novels. They featured British heroes regularly overcoming Germans against impossible odds. A generation of British children, mostly boys, learnt German from these comics and films with similar plots. Sometimes they practised it on real Germans, as did Basil Fawlty in the "war" episode.

trillion-dollar industry. Even in normal times, there was no limit to the number of people with their own unique formula for achieving happiness. There are now professional declutterers who come to your premises and remove all the excess objects that are blocking your path to it. In ancient times, they used to be called burglars.

Since Samuel Smiles (real name) hit the money with <u>Self Help</u> in 1859 entire forests have been cleared for the efforts of his successors. I never thought myself capable of writing a self-improvement book. That sentence may seem ambiguous: make of it what you will. But browsing the competition, I realize that the bar is set pretty low. Authors are coining it from sentiments I would be ashamed to put in a Christmas cracker. "When you want something, all the universe conspires in helping you to achieve it." Puh-lease. The universe never did that to my horse and jockey.

So I am briefly setting aside my autobiography MGHIR! to knock off an uplifting manual. I have a title <u>Destiny Rides Again</u> and I expect soon to fill it with my own blend of gnomic drivel. Here is my first effort: "The glass may be half empty but the next bottle is not even half open." I am too embarrassed to put my name to this, so I shall put the Resident Mouse on the cover under the pseudonym of Charlie Cheese.

7 May

Private Eye publishes a story "Golden Hellers" about a disagreeable affluent family who bear my name, including a Tory party donor knighted for philanthropy. These people are not related to me. If they were, I would not cadge off them. I have asked the journal to point this out in the next edition.

I mentioned a while back that Joseph Heller, for whom I was sometimes mistaken, although not, sadly, by publishers and agents, was not a relative. Nor is Zoe. Nor was Stephen Heller, the nineteenth century Hungarian composer whose pieces are sometimes set to intermediate pianists, although I always found them too pallid for my repertoire and I have never offered them to the neighbours. A heller was a coin of low purchasing power in the old Austro-Hungarian empire and I suspect that is the origin of my family name.

Several previous governments have asked me to assume a peerage and become minister of this, that and everything, but I was playing a lot of cricket then. During a long period of injury I was tempted to accept one of the offers, but only if I could change my name slightly and sit as Lord Helpus. I conveyed this to Garter Principal King of Arms and there was a stuffy silence at the other end of the line: another case of MGHIR!

The Resident Mouse has refused to set his face to my uplifting self-improvement manual, <u>Destiny Rides Again.</u> He wants to publish a volume of pensées of his own. "More likely poncey than pensée," I snapped but he had gone. "You could call it Mouse Droppings", I shouted down the likeliest hole to Noah Fect. MGHIR! I shall do without him. I never really liked the pseudonym of Charlie Cheese, and I might publish DRA under the name of Les Poir. Is that esoteric enough? Books like DRA seem to sell better under mystic-sounding names. I remember the struggling hack writer who was going nowhere under his real name of Jeff Gurdy but did wonderfully well when he rearranged it as Gurdjieff. His mumbo-jumbo is still selling briskly. What can I do with mine? Ricardella? More suitable for pasta. I am stuck on Les Poir.

Prodnose: So what did you want Neil Armstrong to say?

Myself: Can't you see, I'm busy? (To myself) Les Poirot, Hercule's smarter brother? Les Heureux (a musical riposte to the long-running Miserables)? Les Twistagen? Les Ismore?

The Resident Mouse: Could you stop pacing furiously, I can't even hear myself think?

The Foxes: And we can't even fornicate.

8 May

VE Day. Hope the Virus knows this in the Coronabunker. That will tell him what he's taken on. When we've won, as we always do against Johnny Foreigner, I wonder who'll play our leader in the movie. Ah, silly me, Boris Johnson himself.

When he announces our glorious victory he will cut the market for my book of uplifting homilies, so I am rushing ahead with its preparation. Its original title, <u>Destiny Rides Again,</u> is too stately and I shall now be calling it <u>Happy Talk.</u> Then it will get free advertising with every amateur glee club performance of <u>South Pacific.</u> It occurs to me that there might be a market for gloom clubs when all this is over. When the pubs are open again, gloom clubs could meet there for unhappy hours at quarter to three, and listen to each other's sad story they all ought to know.

For my pseudonym, books like <u>Happy Talk</u> seem to sell better with some kind of religious provenance. Perhaps I could become Swami…. Swami…(Sings)

How I love you, how I love you, my dear old Swami... (Pauses. Pauses again. MGHIR!) Or even a Bishop. There was one who used to advertise regularly near Rubato Towers with the splendid name of Bishop Climate.[44] I wonder if Bishop Sunshine is still available. I pull out my Holy Mail Order catalogue for a look-see... look-See... (Pauses.) Bishopric, look-See... (MGHIR!) Sunshine is open, but the rate for bishoprics is ridiculous and would have caused outrage in mediaeval times when the market began. I shall buy a modest pastorship instead and publish <u>Happy Talk</u> as Pastor Isaac Milk. Or should it be Pastor I. Z. Milk? (Paces furiously for several hours, mouse and foxes flee.) Pastor I. Z. Milk for the British edition, Pastor Isaac Milk for the American.

Now for the content. It is terrible to think of an entire book of uplifting sentiments. It's like looking at a hotel minibar with nothing but Kahlua bottles. I seek inspiration from the past. Who was good at keeping up uplift? The nonpareil must be Flann

---

[44] He promised Deliverance From Curses (for a fee) and sold Holy Water, Salt, and Oil at £10 a small portion.

O'Brien's hero, the working-class poet, Jem Casey. I compose a quick quatrain in his style:

"When you've staked your all in life's great race
And finished an also-ran,
When ruin stares you in the face,
A pint of plain is your only man."

This is not quite right for a book like <u>Happy Talk.</u> It is a little too, shall we say, demotic, and it makes far too much sense. Maybe I could nick something from old Jeff Gurdy. Here's one of his zingers: a man may be born, but in order to be born he must first die and in order to die he must first awake. Hmm. I could kick this around, but I notice for the first time that old Gurdy grew the most tremendous moustache. I think you would need one to put over stuff like that.

I remember a very uplifting thing I was told by an early cricket coach: you are the best player of your type in the world. Unfortunately, there is no demand for players of my type anywhere in the world. Nor ever has been. <u>Happy Talk</u> is going to be much harder than I thought.

Prodnose: We're still waiting for what Neil Armstrong should have said.

Myself (Screams): And I'm still busy! (To myself). I know what Coleridge felt about that Person from Porlock.

9 May

I have lost my invisible ink. I suspected the Resident Mouse of nicking my first drafts of Happy Talk for his own volume of cheesy offerings so I took counter-measures. I ordered a large quantity of invisible ink and now I can't see it anywhere.

Happy Talk was delayed yesterday by watching Boris Johnson and the Queen celebrate VE Day. No contest. Boris should stop appearing on the same day as her. It makes him look like the tennis club junior coach on court against Roger Federer. Without breaking the flow of her speech, HM remembered the war against Japan, Boris forgot it, reviving bitter memories of how it was forgotten at the time. Who is writing HM's stuff these days? If it's herself, it's time for her to take out that novel from the desk drawer, although perhaps she was too busy reigning to compose it. She could at least write a few episodes of <u>The Crown</u> on her own, or take a one-person show on the road (she could even call it One). In this form, she could play the old Glasgow Empire on Friday.

Back to <u>Happy Talk.</u> It is a scaly, scary task. I turn for inspiration to my old friend Julie Andrews. It does not help. I can't stand any of her favourite things. A rainy day in a rose garden… kittens being sick all over the carpet… copper kettles you can never get to shine… woollen mittens which get cold and soggy in no time… bad tempered ponies… the neighbours' bratty kids ringing doorbells and running away… wild geese honking all night… And that heavy lumpen menu, schnitzel, noodles, strudels... I try out a few favourite things of my own:

Fresh guacamole and chicken fajitas
With a new jigger of chilled margaritas
Getting at Trump with an insult that stings
These are a few of my favourite things.

Playing the piano and doing it my way,
Getting at Trump again, not in a shy way,
Watching old Prodnose get stung by a bee
These are a few of mes choses favories.

I don't think I'm cut out for <u>Happy Talk.</u> I will leave it to the Resident Mouse and try to corner the opposite market which is certain to revive at the end of lockdown. I have registered the Misery Loves company and will set up a dating service for gloomy people to meet each other in my pub unhappy hours. "Eeyore. NSOH. Interests existential despair. Wants to meet similar for walks in damp places." The great thing about such a dating service is that you can charge both parties double if they don't like each other.

I have been asked if any famous Hellers are related to me. My ancestor, Junker Heller (named after his ricketty pony and trap, they didn't know about vitamin D then which is why the poor pony was ricketty like so many I've backed on the turf) anyway my ancestor Junker Heller played a vital role in lifting the siege of Vienna in 1683. When all seemed lost he persuaded the Turks to break for coffee and that's how we got the croissant. The grateful Holy Roman Emperor Leopold wanted to give him a jump up in the Imperial nobility to graf, but my ancestor scuppered his chances by asking if he could become Graf Paper. My goodness, how he roared!

Prodnose: And the zinger for Neil Armstrong?

Myself: It's a gorgeous day, and there's ever such a lonely bee in the garden.

10 May

One final effort to save Happy Talk. I consult the works of Patience Strong, who delighted a mass audience with her inspirational poetry for over fifty years.[45] Here's a typical couplet: Problems there are bound to be, life can't be all delight
When you think of what went wrong, remember what went right. (The great thing about inspirational verse is that the inspirees don't worry too much about scansion.) That bit of Patience's philosophy has never worked for me. When I drop a catch, all my previous dropped catches appear before me in a mist procession. I nearly drowned once when carried away by the Equator and all my past life started to flash before my eyes. Not only all the dropped catches but all the static horses and dogs and all the rejection letters... I could not take any more and with a mighty effort I was able to trudgeon my way back to the beach at São Tomé e Príncipe.

---

[45] Almost certainly the most published 20th century British poet.

Patience had an amazing secret life which one would love to hear more about. As Vera Bloom she wrote (in just fifteen minutes) the lyrics for the passionate tango "Jealousy", memorably performed by Frankie Laine. I feel another movie coming on, a biopic which would be a fine vehicle for a versatile actor such as Trulie Drenched. By day pretty prude Patience, by night vixen vamp Vera...

To make Happy Talk still more painful, the Resident Mouse is clearly forging ahead with his intended volume of cheesy puffs. I can hear him roaring (within the limits of a rodent) frequently, as I do when I am on a roll. He has taken to wearing a dressing gown made of Turkestan silk, which even in rodent dimensions must have cost ... cost... [punches cliché button] a packet [double punches cliché button] a pretty penny because silkworms in Turkestan don't get out of bed for less than $100 a thread. I recognize it as previously worn by one of his visitors, the dramaturge Terence Ratagain. He is also using Ratagain's cigarette holder. Rubato Towers has strictly no-smoking mouseholes so this is pure affectation. All the creatures here keep to the rules. Even the foxes do not smoke after fornicating, although in a forgotten part of the car park garden I once saw an adder taking a few crafty puffs.

Resident Mouse in the throes of composition

(Later). All is lost. The Resident Mouse is preparing an exercise video to go with his book. I detected squeaky but booming disco music from his hole and a squeaky but booming voice giving out commands. It sounds pretty boring, mostly running in a wheel, but he is trying to exploit the present wartime nostalgia by calling it Wheel Meet Again. That should be all over by the time he brings it out and he might be better off with This Wheel's On Fire, which also would give an easier running pace. That said, wartime nostalgia could easily come back two or three times in the coming year. Nostalgia generally has a much faster cycle these days. One could almost call it Nostalgia Squared: people get nostalgic about the first time they got nostalgic, and celebrate the first time they went to an Eighties tribute band or even first watched a re-run of Happy Days.

Happy Talk is in grave danger of being overtaken and outsold by a homeless mouse, so it is time for Plan C. I will publish a volume called Bah Humbug! under the proud name of Ebenezer Scrooge. It will give expert advice on modern-day thrift, including the avoidance of charity appeals and the precise moment for offering to buy a round of drinks with minimum take-up. Scrooge is due a makeover. If Scrooge transitioned today (as they say in the USA, where death is an obscenity) he would get very respectable obituary coverage: Banker who believed in sound finance and was a pioneer of energy saving and sustainable living.

Prodnose: See you living on gruel! (Sneers)

Myself (loftily): It is very acceptable with Sãotomean chocolate ground over it, and some of my own Grandola and Muscly grains, and on the side a brace of cold snipe with a Bavarian omelette, or umlaut as it's called over there, and if the sturgeons have been laying, a light dusting of the caviar we served to the General on the toasted lime bread, the hand-pounded coffee and order some fresh beans from the estate, I'm sick of has-beans, and I know it's early but perhaps a beakerette of the Glen Dower very special old single-malt whisky ("spirits from the vasty deep were at my nativity") which you'll find in the Not-For-Guests cupboard….

Prodnose: What about the zinger for Neil Armstrong?

Myself: I'm having breakfast now.

<u>11 May</u>

In the hope of keeping Prodnose at bay, here's what Neil Armstrong would have said at the Moon landing had they listened to me. "We have left a footprint which can never be erased." Uplifting and both figuratively and literally true since there is no wind or rain on the Moon. Of course, that was 1969 and I had not allowed for the prospect of space tourism, and Richard Branson galumphing all over the footprint with a reluctant astrohostess in his arms. What progress I shall see in my lifetime, when trippers trash the Moon as they have trashed Everest.

Boris Johnson's speech yesterday reminded me of a David Low Colonel Blimp cartoon from the 1930s: "Gad sir! Mr Baldwin is right. The government has resolved to be guided by the force of circumstances with a firm hand."

Prodnose: Carping again?

Myself: You're back so soon? Have you no essential place of work to walk to in Ultima Thule? (Has sudden epiphany.) But no, Rubato Towers IS your place of work. Your entire mission in life is to goad me. You are the grain of sand that makes me generate my pearls. (Memo to self to send that one to the Journal of Molluscan Studies. Ponders.) Without Prodnose I might have become a mere clam in the shoals of literature. I shall henceforth bear his intrusions for the sake of my art and my public.

Yes, I shall carp and carp for England. One of the most fatal phrases in British history is "Mustn't grumble." It has encouraged the British to accept sub-standard products and services and public agencies and governments, and explains much of our loss of competitiveness. It is the hidden premise of Fawlty Towers: no hotel that awful could survive without the assent of its British guests. One remembers the episode when two Americans check in and bawl out Basil for the lack of a Waldorf salad. They inspire a brief rebellion among the British guests. Even the Major realizes that the hotel is terrible (although others are even worse.) But when the Americans are gone, Basil's rule is restored. In later episodes, he is back snarling "Everything all right?" at the British guests and they obediently assent.

The only thing that will stop me is that others are carrying the carping torch. It burns brightly and is being relayed by willing hands. In just a few short hours it has become otiose for me to carp about the meaningless Stay Alert! slogan (for what? And if I see Johnny Virus lurking at a street corner do I have a go against him myself or leave it to the Home Guard?), or about the insouciant instruction to get to work without public transport, or about the lack of preparation and guidance for employers in making safe their workplaces and work processes. Keep that going, Starmer. Carry On Carping! They should have made a film of it in the classic series, with Sid James as Sir Sidney Sidemouth and Kenneth Williams as Fu-Kyu, the Mandarin Moaner of Wing-Jing.[46]

I am concerned that thousands of people will try to get to their former place of work to maintain the pretence that they are essential to it. I am even more concerned that distancing regulations will destroy the social life that makes so many offices bearable for their inmates, and whose organization provides a harmless outlet for so many otherwise useless (punches euphemism button) alternately gifted employees. Deprived of the office time they would otherwise spend getting birthday cards signed, collecting the tea money or managing collective outings, these people might try to do some actual work and this could be very damaging

---

[46] The Carry On films were a highly popular low budget comedy series, with broad "seaside postcard humour" and many silly names. The actors Sid James and Kenneth Williams were regular performers.

to the business concerned. Perhaps they will be asked to supervise handwashing, or assigned to the good works in the community which businesses do to distract people from their real mission of making money by grinding the faces of the poor. Some might be asked to run academy schools.[47]

12 May

Happy birthday to my all-time idol Steve Winwood. I was told years ago that I was once in the same room as him but I had not known at the time and was unable to fall on my knees and kiss the hem of his garment.

The Resident Mouse kept me awake all night with a party to celebrate a publisher's advance for his little nosegay of uplifting homilies. The racket was worse than the fornicating foxes, worse even than a sea urchin orgy. His book is to be called <u>Keep Squeaking Through</u>, but the French edition will be

---

[47] Publicly funded schools not run by public authorities but private corporations or trusts, modelled on charter schools in the USA. A pet wheeze of Tony Blair's administration.

published with arty typography as <u>Les Sourires
d'un Souris.</u> The publisher is Little Brown, and I am
certain they chose him because he is both of these
things. His advance was paid in ripe Camembert,
and he had it piped directly into his mousehole in
Rubato Towers. Well, really! Did he think I would
purloin the fruits of his honest toil?

I do not begrudge him his moments of joy. I know
what is in store for him. The desperate struggle to
explain his very best jests to a baffled editor and
preserve them for publication. The equally
desperate struggle over the choice of the author's
photograph. Accepting the publicist's orders to be
interviewed for insomniacs and Swedish sailors on
the graveyard shift of Radio Nowhere, and to
attend signings in Snaresbrook, trying desperately
to remember there the name he has been told only
seconds before, hitting on the ingenious device of
asking the buyer to spell it, and being told "Mother.
I did say it was for her." And before he even knows
it, the first heartbreaking sight of his book on a pile
of remainders. Heh-heh.

In its partial and confused relaxations on sport, the government has wisely decided not to re-open public swimming pools. This is not because of Johnny Virus, although I suspect that he loves swimming and they would have to pump the waters full of Donald Trump's leftover bleach. I am more concerned with the possibility that thousands of parents have been boasting to their children in lockdown about their past triumphs on the high diving board and would be compelled to put these to the proof.

The government is apparently allowing swimming in lakes and rivers but they will have first to remove the jellyfish and Sir Philip Green.

<u>13 May</u>

One or two of my public, that is to say half of them, confessed themselves flummoxed by my mention three days ago of Glen Dower very special old single-malt whisky ("spirits from the vasty deep were at my nativity"). It might have been a bit delphic or sibylline or even obscure. I was trying to refer to Shakespeare's only half-way decent gag.

It comes in King Henry the Fourth part 1, when the Welsh rebel Owen Glendower meets Harry Hotspur, the gifted striker for Tottynghamme. Shakespeare was an English chauvinist who would have voted for Nigel Farage and he was happy to insult the Welsh by caricaturing one of their national heroes as a windy boaster about his paranormal gifts. He is taunted by the commonsense English Hotspur (now exactly the sort of chap we need in the fight against Johnny Virus.) Glendower gets more and more peeved and eventually exclaims "I can call spirits from the vasty deep", setting up Hotspur to reply "Why, so can I, or so can any man But will they come when you do call for them?"

Did I detect a fluttered eyelid, or the soupçon of a smirk? I said it was only half-way decent. And it is Shakespeare's best effort. He was lucky to have a public that liked tragedies and histories because his comic writing is terrible. A few bits of slapstick are all right but his comic patter would defeat even a master performer like Donald Trump. I cannot believe that audiences ever laughed at Shakespeare's clowns even when they understood what they meant. I think Shakespeare wrote them in to help the Globe sell ice creams and soft drinks when they came on. The worst is Touchstone. Tombstone would be a better name, considering all the actors who have died in the part. For that matter, As You Like It should be renamed Please Yourselves, Frankie Howerd's woebegone response when one of his lame gags failed to produce a titter.

Here's some of the material Shakespeare gave to Touchstone, when he is wooing Audrey the goat-girl, his hapless feed. "I am here with thee and thy goats as the most capricious poet, honest Ovid, was among the Goths." It's ghastly, even when the actor pronounces Goths in the Elizabethan way, as Goaths, and even when he labours the word capricious to remind the audience that it originally meant goat-like (as in Capricorn, geddit?) And as for

Touchstone's riff a bit further on: "Courage! As horns are odious, they are necessary. It is said 'many a man knows no end of his goods.' Right! Many a man has good horns and knows no end of them. Well, that is the dowry of his wife; 'tis none of his own getting. Horns? Poor men alone? No, no, the noblest deer hath them as huge as the rascal." Er… Leave your name, but not with us.

I wonder if Shakespeare's original Touchstone had some kind of visual aid to work with, giant sandals, or a beard with nesting birds, or hose which fell down to reveal a giant revolving codpiece. It is hard to tell because Shakespeare did not leave behind many stage directions. The best known (even to Bertie Wooster) is "Exit, pursued by a bear." And it was a real bear! Shakespeare was paid to stick him into The Winter's Tale by a bear keeper to promote his star turn. The bear did not just pursue Antigonus, he pursued him on a unicycle while playing a lute. The talented bear's name was Cymbeline and Shakespeare wrote a whole play for him. His performance in the title role would have made it more bearable than anyone since. Bearable. MGHIR!

14 May

A topical musical interlude. My thanks to Mick Hodgkin for the first two lines and the inspiration to continue.

Summer No Holiday

We're not going on a summer holiday
No more travel until '22
Fun and laughter but they're all now memories:
Lots of worries for me and you
For a week or fifty-two.

We're watching where the sun shines brightly
We're watching where the sea is clear,
We're watching them on the movies
That we made when we went last year.

Lots of people having long summer holidays
In a place they never wanted to
Locked together on a summer holiday

With no way to make their dreams come true
And the kids are stuck too
With me and you.

Original by Brian Bennett and Bruce Welch

Some of my public may not have seen the original performance on film by Cliff Richard and the Shadows in their heyday. Is there an antonym to heyday, which invariably follows? Possibly Mayday, and can one experience it without ever having a heyday? Do descents imply a peak? Asking on behalf of a friend.

14 May (later)

Our leader and skipper is fond of sporting metaphors so here's a new one for him: Johnny Virus is still at the batting crease but we've got all our fielders in the right places and we've slowed his rate of scoring…

A Chorus of Carpers: … did not have proper practice nets… hasn't a clue… chasing the ball …

no idea how to get him out… just hoping the Virus will declare….

I knew I would be asked what happened to Cymbeline, Shakespeare's performing bear.

Like many others before and since, Cymbeline had his head turned by his early performing success in The Winter's Tale. He dismissed the keeper who had taught him everything since he had first mimed to Teddy Bears Picnic, and acquired a servile entourage of personal trainers, writers, agents, publicists, chefs, and fur cleaners. He demanded endless rewrites from Shakespeare to showcase him. Thanks to Cymbeline, there are no fewer than 543 bears in Shakespeare's plays, apart from the one which introduced him to his adoring public. He demanded cast changes. A teenage boy was no longer good enough for his Cleopatra and he insisted on Ingrid Beargman. Foolishly, he started giving notes to Shakespeare's established leading man, Richard Burbage (who steadfastly refused to spell his name Bearbage), and even more foolishly he began to upstage him.

Like many others before and since, Cymbeline went too far. He upstaged Burbage delivering Hamlet's famous soliloquy. There are three bears in it. There were nearly five but Shakespeare clung to a shred of his dignity as a writer and refused to open it "To bear or not to bear."

On Burbage's first mention of bear, "For who would bear the whips and scorns of time", Cymbeline unicycled across the stage strumming the new instrument invented for him, the lutelele. Burbage had to pause and wait for the groundlings to subside.

On his second mention of bear, "Who would these fardels bear" Cymbeline unicycled across the stage while juggling some early season quince. Burbage had to pause again and wait for the groundlings to subside.

On his third mention of bear, "...puzzles the will and makes us rather bear...", Cymbeline did the unicycling upside down and juggled the quince with his feet. Burbage stormed off the stage, vowing revenge.

Burbage was shrewd enough not to challenge Cymbeline to a duel. Against a cycling bear with a personal trainer, he knew that he would stand no chance, being fat and out of breath, as Shakespeare had to say in the script when he could not get a stunt double for Burbage in Hamlet's duel scene. Burbage had a much better scheme of revenge, using his expert knowledge of actors and their vanity.

He persuaded Cymbeline to play the part of Falstaff in a double-header of King Henry the Fourth parts 1 and 2. Cymbeline agreed, after Shakespeare made a few script changes, including a new closing scene in which Falstaff rejects Prince Hal and takes the throne himself by acclamation. Shakespeare makes Falstaff gulp sack, fortified white wine, almost continuously (he made good money from product placement in his plays and had an arrangement with a local wine importer), and this survived the script changes he made for Cymbeline. Most actors used coloured water for their gulps, but Burbage urged Cymbeline to try out the newly introduced school of Ye Methodde acting and to inhabit and become Falstaff rather than just perform him. To this end, he induced Cymbeline to drink real sack for several days and nights before the performance – as the real Falstaff would have done.

The results were predictable. Cymbeline made his first appearance, bestriding two unicycles at once and slicing the quince in mid air with a sharp sword. He was almost immediately overcome. Dropping the sharp sword, which luckily for him rolled into the wings, he collapsed onto the stage insensible. At first the groundlings howled, thinking it was part of the act. But when they saw Cymbeline inert and unresponsive to prompts they grew understandably restive. They actually set fire to the Globe theatre and the entire company had to move to the nearby Artichoke. But without

Cymbeline. He was dismissed with ignominy and ig nomoney. This episode is the origin of the otherwise inexplicable expression, giving someone the sack.

Cymbeline still had a hefty Elizabethan fortune from his acting career and he tried to make it work for him. But like many others before and since, the ex-actor had little head for business. His first ill-fated business venture was an open-air shopping precinct in Stratford-on-Avon, but no other investors were willing to risk their money in a Bear Market. Then he set up a chain of burger restaurants known as Ye Bear Grylls.[48] But this failed because Sir Walter Raleigh had not yet discovered the potato and the restaurants could not serve any fries.

Cymbeline was down and out. His entourage deserted him, having first pillaged his assets including the unicycle, quinces and sword. All he

---

[48] Bear Grylls is Britain's Chief Scout and features in a popular televised survival series.

had left was the lutelele. He stood pitifully in alleyways, strumming <u>Streets Of London</u>, and believe me, it sounded as dire then as it does now. His last remaining fan (shared with an ancestor of mine) found him and gave him some good news. There was a vacancy for a staff position with the Earl of Warwick, and if he scurried Cymbeline could reach the Earl before he had finished the interviews. Cymbeline handed over the lutelele and duly scurried. In all his misfortunes he had kept his looks and his presence – and the Earl duly gave him the staff position without an interview. Cymbeline imagined that he would become a Secretary when that really mattered, as Thomas Cromwell to Henry VIII or Ye Efficient Baxter who was then terrorizing the contemporary Earl of Emsworth at the original Blandings Castle.

But the Earl had meant staff position in a literal sense. He wanted someone to carry his famous ragged staff, which was part of his family crest.

It was a distinct comedown for the fallen idol. But he took the job and did it so well that he was incorporated into the Earl's coat of arms. Happily, that made him immortal when the Earl's arms passed into other hands (so to say.) When county cricket is restored to us, watch Warwickshire and admire the handsome bear on their caps and shirts. That is the great Cymbeline.

15 May

They tell me the economic situation is so bad that the Queen has put the country into Prince Philip's name. I detected some modest roaring, probably because that is not one of my jests. It is recycled from the historic advice to King George V by his favourite Cabinet Minister, J H (Jimmy) Thomas, during the crash of 1931, to put the country into Queen Mary's name. Long before professional image-building, Thomas established himself as a comic working-class cheeky chappie, remembering to drop his Hs even in formal evening wear. He kept up his act even when he abandoned the Labour party to join the National Government in 1931. His jest was his biggest contribution to history, which has not given him a very good press. He is the only Cabinet Minister to have appointed himself an England Test cricket selector, but that story is for my podcast public.

I asked the Queen if she had any memories of Thomas at our last audience together, when we performed all her favourite songs by Britney Spears and her sister Asparagus. She could not remember any other jests from him, but she asked if his leader, Ramsay MacDonald ever finished the funny story he began to tell her at Balmoral in 1930.[49] HM has heard jests from every British Prime Minister since Stanley Baldwin and I urged her to place them all in the National Collections. She gave a ... (punches cliché button) a sad little smile. "I'd have a job with Mrs Thatcher." I sympathized readily. Mrs Thatcher was a nightmare to her gag-writer, the playwright Ronald (Ronnie) Millar. He gave her some wonderful material. "You turn if you want to. The lady's not for turning." Joan Rivers would have died for that gag. Mrs Thatcher died with it. She made it as unfunny as Shakespeare's clowns.

---

[49] British Labour party leader and Prime Minister 1924, 1929-31. Formed and led National (nonLabour) Government 1931-35. Famous for windy rhetoric with never-ending sentences.

HM has made many wonderful jests herself, most of them distinctly on the raunchy side. She has made me roar regularly in our regular sessions over the Scrabble board. She nearly always wins, and I have learnt painfully never to challenge the words she puts down, especially those with high-value letters (she alone is allowed to put down QUEEN). If my vocabulary seems sometimes un peu recherché that is all her fault.

The Queen is the most wonderful mimic (she can even do Chris Grayling[50]) but not as good as her sister. Peter Cook never listened to Harold Macmillan to prepare his famous imitation. He cribbed it straight from Princess Margaret.[51] Fact.

---

[50] A widely derided recent Cabinet minister, almost devoid of personality and therefore a stern test for mimics.

[51] The great and original comedian Peter Cook achieved national fame by mimicking the then Prime Minister, Harold Macmillan, in the groundbreaking revue Beyond The Fringe in 1960. He was in the Princess Margaret "set" of actors and artists and café society members, and was rumoured to have had an affair with her.

16 May

Our fearless leader, now wrestling Johnny Virus to the floor, now wants his MPs back in the House of Commons to bay at Keir Starmer. Like some movie star on the slide after a run of turkeys who desperately needs his entourage around him. Like poor old Elvis Presley in his later years at Las Vegas, who needed his backing singers to do the high notes for him. I saw Elvis not long ago outside my local supermarket. He was riding Shergar[52]. But I did not have time to give them my autograph.

There is no need for any MPs to crawl in person to their party leaders in the House of Commons. The place is insanitary enough without them. If Premier League footballers can perform without live fans, a park player like Boris Johnson should be able to do the same. Has he never heard of canned applause? The technology's been around for years, and it would easily permit faraway fawning and socially-distant sycophancy.

---

[52] A famous racehorse, kidnapped in 1983 and never seen again.

In fairness to Boris Johnson, he is not the first to need a claque at Prime Minister's Questions. Tony Blair was the worst. He never liked the House of Commons and he never went there without arranging one in advance, a case of clunk-claque every trip.[53]

It would be easier to replace toadying MPs with Alexa. She could ask a Question at PMQs in the normal way ("Number 5. Sir"). The Prime Minister would give the normal meaningless replay ("I have been in a meeting") and then say "Alexa, ask me supplementary number 5") and she would say "May I congratulate my Right Honourable Friend on his recent visit to Dudbury and did he hear my constituents' hearts throbbing with joy after his speech?" Alexa could get through many more such questions than live MPs, but it might drive her crazy. MPs go through years of conditioning to become lobotomized lobbyfodder. A few don't last the course and retain career-threatening symptoms of independence and critical thought. Alexa, with

---

[53] A long-running campaign to use car seatbelts: clunk-click every trip.

her fierce if artificial intelligence, might well be the same way. She could easily flip out at Prime Minister's Questions. She might suddenly blurt "Listen, fatty, I've seen plastic waste that could do a better job than you. I'm taking over."

Alexa would be a very popular Prime Minister. There would be no need for elections: voters could tell her directly what they wanted. The ultimate in taking back control. "Alexa, save the NHS" or "Alexa, clean the air" or "Alexa, rebalance the economy on a basis of neo-classical endogenous growth." Has anyone yet asked Alexa to wipe out the virus?

17 May

If we cannot have Alexa to run our government, perhaps we could ask a guest Prime Minister from another country. If we were really lucky, we might get Jacinda Ardern of New Zealand. It would be salutary for all political leaders to have to offer themselves for selection by another country at regular intervals. Boris Johnson might hear the terrible words I used to hear when teams were picked on the school playground: no, it's your turn to have him.

It might be too difficult to organize a job swop of major world leaders. After all, several of them cannot leave their countries for fear of arrest. Peter Tatchell is ready to pounce on them[54], even if the International Criminal Court is too cumbersome. Perhaps there could be regular multinational opinion polls to establish which leaders might be popular, or even recognized, in other countries. It's a fair guess that Donald Trump would get heavily negative ratings almost everywhere – but unfortunately this would probably boost his hold on his own supporters in the United States. Trump would certainly take it as a triumph that he has made America as hated abroad as in its great days. It might well do more harm to him electorally to show that he is loved by foreigners, but this would

---

[54] Gay rights activist who bravely tried to achieve a citizen's arrest of Zimbabwe's despot, Robert Mugabe.

be beyond the capacity of present Fake News Generators.

The latest polls leave me worried that Trump may actually be impervious to Fake News. After all, he has proved impervious to reality. The Democrats may need a stronger candidate than my old friend Joe Biden, so I asked my other old friend Michelle Obama if she might be willing to be drafted. (You read it here first!)

Of course people would ask what role her husband would play in her administration, as the First Gentleman. Some American states have 2-term limits for office holders, and historically this was sometimes circumvented by the retiring man running his wife as the replacement candidate with himself as an adviser to the "little lady" in office. I do not think Michelle would accept such a role.

Years ago on one of my American coast-to-coast tours (I walked out of Caesar's Palace when they failed to provide the right sort of lime for my post-performance margarita and have never been back since) someone told me the story of one of these "little ladies" who was duly elected and appointed her rascally, cheating husband as her adviser on a salary of $1 a year. She discovered in office that she had the power to grant divorces. She gave herself one, and ruled the state with her lover. The husband kept the $1 salary, she and the lover enjoyed the official salary and whatever else they could make out of her job. I have not yet been able to confirm whether this story is true. It really should be, it would make a great movie.

18 May

I have apologized to the Resident Mouse for interrupting the composition of his uplifting volume <u>Keep Squeaking Through.</u> I had one of my "bad turns", feverishly pacing Rubato Towers, bawling incoherent oaths, and smashing the remains of the inferior crockery I keep for the VAT inspector.[55] Nothing against the VAT inspector, but

---

[55] A ghastly British sales tax which afflicts even authors

I think it would be impolitic to show him the Sèvres originals I use for my elevenses.

Only Mandelson can affect me this way. I don't mean the pitiful little virus that used to annoy me. Call yourself a virus? Listen, the NHS has just moved my next appointment to deal with you to October. That's all they think of you as a virus. There are split toenails getting priority over you, Mandelson. No. I mean the real one, insofar as real can be applied to such a protean figure as Peter Mandelson. I long ago barred him from actual admittance to Rubato Towers. I showed his image to the foxes and they kindly agreed to suspend fornicating to bite him should he set foot in the grounds. Unfortunately, news stories about Mandelson can give me a "bad turn" remotely. And this story produced one of my worst turns since I auditioned unsuccessfully at the Oldham Orpheum. Mandelson is a candidate to become the next director-general of the World Trade Organization. It is a job carrying money and power, and countless opportunities to place his smirking features and condescending utterances into the world's media. (Begins to shake, Resident Mouse prudently extracts piano key and locks the instrument.)

I thanked the little chap and explained myself to him over some cheese nibbles. Fortunately he does not like pineapple with them any more than I do. Who invented this combination, which made the Seventies such a lost decade? The Resident Mouse's great-to-the-tenth grandparents were not even born when I first started to loathe Peter Mandelson, so it took a long time. When I had finished the little chap had turned ashen. It is hard to tell when a mouse turns ashen, but believe me he was ashener than when I told him about the Great Tea Trolley Disaster of 1967,[56] ashener even than after hearing of the events surrounding the run-out of Jeffrey Archer.

I will spare readers the full Mandelson dossier I have just sent to my new friend Keir Starmer, who has made such a cracking start as Labour leader

---

[56] See above for March 28

before he has even used any of the brand-new jests I gave him. I will mention only Mandelson's account (on the website of his secretive consultancy) of a delightful tea party with Mr Hsi, the Paramount Brute running China. Mandelson praises Mr Hsi's extraordinary calm, although it is easy for him to be calm when he can have any critic banged up indefinitely in a gulag or psychiatric institution. During the 1930s, there was a repellent journalist called George Ward Price, special correspondent of the <u>Daily Mail</u>. He produced a book called <u>I Know These Dictators,</u> which boasted of the meals he had shared with Mussolini and Hitler (I think they even carried recipes). Ward Price eventually recanted in 1939, when Hitler swallowed what was left of Czechoslovakia, but Mandelson has yet to withdraw anything he has said or done about China or Russia (where he served as a non-executive director of the Sistema Group, one of Putin's top defence contractors).

There are many other politicians who make me feel that standards no longer matter in British politics (Boris Johnson is only the latest) but Peter

Mandelson was the first, and he represents unfinished business. He told hundreds of other people how to behave in British politics but he never took any responsibility for the impact of his own behaviour, never considered what it might have done to make voters despise their government and their governing class.

The Resident Mouse has promised to mobilize all his chums in a mass squeak of protest if Mandelson gets the WTO post. Most kind of him, but I fear this will be missed. Knowing Mandelson, he might even arrange for the announcement to coincide with one of the collective clappings for the NHS workers, which would at least offer the piquant spectacle of Jeremy Corbyn appearing to applaud his elevation. (As was once said in France of two members of Napoleon III's family: not even their hatred of one another could endear them to the nation.)

So I am asking all my readers who are registered British voters to write to their MPs to urge them to act against Mandelson's appointment. Or write direct to the International Trade Secretary, Liz Truss. Restrain your astonishment that she is the longest-serving Cabinet minister in Boris Johnson's collection. Tell her instead that her reputation in British politics, which now soars on the Maeonian wing, will sink into a Sargasso Sea of stagnant mockery...

Prodnose: What are you on today? And can I try some?

Myself (in a trance) ... into a Stygian vortex of mephitic derision if this privileged puffball were to be promoted on her watch.

Feeling better now.

19 May

My daily to-do list was crowded enough.

One: defeat Trump

Two: induce remorse in Boris Johnson

Three: raise English prose to heights never before attempted, let alone achieved

Four: ditto English light verse

Five: prepare cricketing podcasts with Peter Oborne for global public. (You would be surprised how much writing and rehearsal is necessary for a freewheeling conversation.)

Six: polish silver bibelots.

Seven: remove persistent spot of mould in bathroom

Eight: rehearse the zombie, the zamboni, the zooter, the zorker (continues page 94782) in front of full-length mirror with running commentary and Pakistan crowds chanting "wah-wah"

Nine: consider interesting email offers from Nigeria

Ten: attempt sneak peek at Squeak manuscript by the Resident Mouse.

And now I must add Eleven: frustrate Mandelson. Sighs. Must this cup pass to me? Could I not withdraw my resistance and let him assume the office of Director-General of the World Trade Organization? It's not as if anyone had heard of the outgoing DG or any of his predecessors. They are like all those Kings of Israel and Judah who get a one-sentence wrap-up in the Old Testament, remembered by no one except Bertie Wooster in his lone academic prize for Scripture Knowledge. Mandelson might be relatively harmless in this position. When he was EU Trade Commissioner one read about him only in the context of the Chinese Knicker Crisis. He issued stern warnings against the Chinese for making so many knickers, not only wrecking the elasticity of demand for European knickers but creating a knock-on effect for the European gusset industry. He had no impact in the job, indeed one could say he was pants...

No. For shame! I must not falter or fail. I cannot ignore Mandelson any more than I can leave the mould in the bathroom. It is a very small patch. It would be easy to conceal it under the soap dish. But left unchecked it would spread everywhere, rendering my bath unusable and ruining the hot asses' milk. It is my duty to scrub Mandelson, to remove him not only from power but from attention, so that not even his friendships with Oleg Derepaska or Jeffrey Epstein can secure him any mention in the media. I see him trying to reinvent himself as an entertainer, like Horatio Bottomley[57] in his last years, begging for the opportunity to open a discount warehouse in Lower Dudbury, and losing the gig to a singing goldfish. Then, only then, will my life's work be complete.

20 May

As a full-time journalist I always had the ambition of receiving a Carter-Ruck letter, named after the then legal rottweilers to the famous, threatening to sue me for something I had written. It was a red letter day when I actually landed one ... our client most gravely defamed... utterly unjustifiable ... will seek restitution to the uttermost farthing of your possessions (and your cat's) ... demand retraction and the most humble and abject apology

---

[57] Hugely popular Trumpian journalist and MP in UK in Great War era, imprisoned for fraud, failed comeback in music halls on release

with tears of contrition ... we know where you live... Of all things, it was for a book review, in which I had quoted accurately the author's accurate statements that his subject (now dead) was a crook and a friend of Prince Charles.

One does not hear the name of Carter-Ruck so often these days. I do hope they have not fallen on hard times. It was some inferior firm of barratreers who sent me an admonitory letter injuncting my forthcoming autobiography <u>My Goodness How I Roared!</u> on behalf of a Certain Personage. They had obtained not only just some run of the mill injunction but one of the new state-of-the-art ones which bars me from naming the Personage or his or her gender by birth or self-selection, or nationality, or tax domicile, or star sign, or the judge who granted it, or the premises in which it was granted now serving as a court and whether the judge washed judicial hands properly in adequate facilities before granting it, and what was the weather like at the time. In all fairness, I will say that the Personage was not Peter Mandelson. I may be taking a risk, but hey, that's the kind of guy I am.

The barratreers alleged that I intended to defame the Personage in question. I replied in rem and in personam. I have no formal legal qualifications but as a former Gold Medallist at the Institute of Tortfeasors and Champertists I know how to deal with these people. "Sirs, I had not intended to mention your client in my autobiography, and if I did it would be only to find an outlet for insults I had not been able to use elsewhere. You will be aware that insults, however colourful, do not constitute defamation, which is the allegation of facts likely to diminish your client's reputation among right-thinking people. It would greatly improve your client's reputation among right-thinking people if they believed your [unidentified genderless] client to have once been among my acquaintance." That should settle their dreary and tepid hash, although I have little optimism that they will pay my bill, based on very reasonable hourly rates. "To opening your letter 50 gns… to stamping your letter and placing it in file 75 gns…

to perusal of your letter 120 gns...
disbursements.... refreshers... viaticums..."

21 May

I managed to sneak an oblique peek at the chic Squeak manuscript of fashionable uplift from the Resident Mouse.

I have to say that some of his stuff was distinctly passable if you can stand that sort of thing. "When life leaves you in the mud, be a hippopotamus. When your boss has you on the carpet, turn it into a magic one and fly to your enchanted place." Enchanted, by gum, not just happy, he must have learnt how to use the advanced cliché button. "Why expect the worst and get bad news twice over?" Why indeed? It almost makes you think. And here's a real zinger: "Act for others, think for yourself."

Just a moment. That's one of mine. He's been stealing my best stuff for his dismal confection. I summoned the mousecreant to my chambers. He confessed all. He's been listening to me talk in my sleep.

Well, never in my wildest dreams did I imagine myself spouting spoonfuls of sugar in my sleep. Beats there somewhere under the wry world-weary railer of Rubato Towers the soppy heart of a panda-lover? When put to the test, might I fail to laugh at the death of Little Nell?

It poses a knotty legal problem which I might put to my lawyers if I had any to represent me. Even ambulance chasers have spurned my proposals to litigate. Are words uttered unconsciously subject to copyright? Or do they constitute an offer to the world in general? And what about the crazed wisdom one sometimes heard in public transport when Boris Johnson allowed people to use it? I go to my law library and consult <u>Every Boy's Guide To Piracy</u>. I remember being very disappointed in the contents when I first acquired it from hoarded pocket money but they have served me well in later life. I gather that the author has made a fortune from the Chinese editions, but unfortunately he can't get at it.

The tome is silent on my problem. So are Wisden Cricketers Almanack and my collections of the Journal of Molluscan Studies. I have therefore reached a private agreement with the rodent author. He will read back to me any of my apnoeistic aphorisms before using them and I will hold back any which might be useful to my private clients. Anything else, he can melt into his cheesy fondu. (Fondu at last, as Mr Stanley said to Mr Livingstone. MGHIR!)

21 May

I have received a plea from my public for a song based on apnœistic aphorisms. Anything to please so here is one (and with the ligature this time.)

Apnœistic aphorisms got me aglow,
Those apnœistic aphorisms I deliver,
Sparky observations and endless bon mots
Flowing through my dreams just like a river.

Each morning I wake up in a heap
(Never snoring, simply roaring)
And hear the gags I've made in my sleep.
Such zingers!

When it gets inspired
My subconscious won't stop
But now I'm feeling wired
And always running.

Going crazy, God knows,
And over the top:
Wish I could be Prodnose
And give up punning.

Please let me make it through tonight
Without a jest:
Apnœistic aphorisms
Please would you give me a rest?

The Gershwins did not make it easy with their short lines and it will need an accomplished patterist to deliver my version.

23 May

A Mouse Writes: my landlord and literary tutor Richard Heller regrets that he is unable to join you today. He has had a repeat visit from Mandelson the Mystery Virus, after a long and welcome absence, and will be spending most of the weekend asleep. He expects to resume the struggle to eject Mandelson from the body politic and his own. Since you are asking, I think he would enjoy any selections from the cheese range at Fortnum and Mason. In his absence, perhaps you will enjoy a few selections from my forthcoming book <u>Keep Squeaking Through.</u>

The stars may be receding at the speed of light, but you can always reach Planet Content.

Be true to yourself. Your conscience has no resale value.

Lies are like lilies. The sweeter they smell, the faster they wither. But the truth is a cactus.

These are mine, not leftovers from Richard. Mandelson made him say some strange things last night. Can you defame someone in sleep and is there a defence of fair reporting?

<u>24 May</u>

A Mouse Writes Again: Richard Heller regrets that he is still unable to replenish the golden treasury of English prose owing to the recrudescence (his word) of Mandelson, his Mystery Virus. I offer all his devastated public a few additional cheering selections from my book <u>Keep Squeaking Through.</u>

The hardest miles are easy if you start them with the S.

When the milk of life goes sour, be patient. Before you know, it will be cheese.

A dog barks at the Moon. Another dog joins it, and another. Soon hundreds of dogs are baying into the night. The Moon shines on and rises in the sky. When your world is full of baying dogs, be the Moon.

Humble, but mine own again. Richard had a better night but one without aphorisms. He appeared to believe in his sleep that he was bowling again and bamboozling a series of the world's greatest batsmen. The foxes complained about one of his appeals.

<u>25 May</u>

A Mouse Writes Again... Oh no, he doesn't. I'm back. Actually feeling a lot worse after a sleepless night with Mandelson the Mystery Virus, but from long experience in cricket and literature I know the fickleness of the public. It is a big risk to leave the twelfth man for too long in one's place. Admit it, some of you were looking forward to a new instalment of mousy mush. One more day and he'd have become insufferable. Already he was starting to refer to my residence as Rodento Towers. The idea.

I had intended to write about Seven Days in May and thanks to Mandelson's visit I now have only six of them. I am getting another summons to a fevered unrefreshing nap but I shall return.

(Later) Now then. Seven Days In May. Political thriller of early 60s. Made into movie. Liberal President (Frederic March) makes arms treaty with Soviet Union. Popular charismatic patriotic general, chairman of Joint Chiefs of Staff (Burt Lancaster) fiercely opposed forms military cabal to seize government. Frustrated by loyal Marine colonel (Kirk Douglas) with unnecessary but still lovely help from ex-mistress (Ava Gardner). President is saved. Apologies for breathless style, like Tony Blair at his worst. Blame Mandelson virus. (Takes deep draught of old Glen Ford very special single-malt whisky: "it's dependable.")

The movie was resisted by the Pentagon but received secret help to gain access to authentic locations on the orders of President Kennedy, who did not trust his generals. Sadly, he never got to see the released version.

I have written a remake. The President is borderline deranged. He is coherent only when he is lying. He either cannot or will not read important documents. He ingests untested drugs. He is enraged by questioning, never mind contradiction. He encourages armed mobs to threaten opposing state governments. To help him win a second term, millions of likely voters for his challenger are being kept off the register for weird reasons or told to risk death if they do go out to vote. Of course, this will need careful exposition to make it believable.

Exposition is the toughest job for us in the screen trade, whether masters or humble apprentices. In the 30s they managed with a hangover from silent movies – a big placard setting out the premise of the plot "1588 and King Philip of Spain has sent his mighty Armada to conquer England from Queen Elizabeth. But her top admiral, Frank Drake, is calmly lining up a strike in his local bowling alley". This gave way in the 1950s to You Mean? dialogue, especially in sci-fi movies. A ditzy assistant (usually blonde female but just occasionally eager teenage boy) would ask "You mean?..." and have the plot explained by the hero: "That's right, Janet (or Chip), we're being invaded by giant squidlike creatures from Neptune." This technique in turn became clichéd and mocked, but for this movie I think it could be profitably revived. "That's right, Janet, the President of the United States is a dingbat."

26 May

A Mouse Writes .... Thank you, Mr Mate. I'll take the wheel for this passage. Yes, I am sure. (Mouse leaves reluctantly). I know I don't look at my best after another sleepless bout with Mandelson, the Mystery Virus. I shall probably be asleep for the rest of the day, and if the little chap gets past my new defences who knows what molasses he will drip onto my public in my name?

But I want to say why Boris Johnson is starting to remind me of Nixon. Far-fetched, of course. Nixon had far more ability. But first, Nixon wasted a lot of political capital defending unelected aides whom nobody liked. Second, what brought Nixon down was that Congressional Republicans started to sound stupid when they defended him to their constituents. Enough of them found this experience humiliating and frightening to desert Nixon.

Dominic Cummings has now made Tory MPs look stupid to their locked-down constituents. Some have broken ranks already. Many others may not know yet how stupid they sound defending him. MPs of all parties these days get years of specialized training in delivering a message without knowing how stupid they look. They may well be rewarded for this, as Minister for Bubbleblowing or Shadow Spokesman on Suet. But eventually reality bites. MPs in lockdown are not in the House of Commons all day surrounded by each other. Although remotely, they are now in much deeper contact with their constituents – real people who expect a real person to serve them, not a party bot. When they put the frighteners on enough Tory MPs over Cummings, Johnson is burnt toast. (Why, incidentally, does the stock cliché refer to toast alone? Toast is something people want and like. It gets thrown away when it is burnt beyond scraping, or just possibly, found to be mouldy despite toasting. I have told those responsible for the cliché button.)

They wrote an opera about Nixon after his fall. Will they do the same for Johnson? It would have to be an opera bouffe.

27 May

A Mouse Writes Again: My landlord Richard Heller had another disturbed night with the Mystery Virus he named after Peter Mandelson, a person who has not made my acquaintance. Richard appeared to believe that he was on the lime plantation on his private island in São Tomé e Príncipe and it would have been cruel for me to wake him. He is now gargling in preparation for his podcast public, so perhaps his literary public might appreciate a few more uplifting morsels – or should I say, mousels? (protracted squoars (squeaky roars)) – from my forthcoming book.

When your life has jumped on the wrong bus, have you thought of changing your destination?

If you wait to be certain, you may miss the chance to be right.

To you it may be a thistle, but to Eeyore it's lunch.

I am going to add handy household hints to my book, including the many I have learnt as Richard's unwaged cleaner. Here's today's top tip. A piece of mouldy bread is an ideal way to remove stains from wallpaper.

Myself: Unwaged? A calumny. He gets free lodging, free literary tuition even in my sleep, constant cheese, and all my failed granola. And who provided him with the mouldy bread? But I never knew about his top tip. They must have done a thorough job of finishing Rubato Towers in the 1890s if they wallpapered all the mouseholes.

28 May

In my distant schooldays I read Jonathan Swift for English A Level. I read him again intermittently for pleasure and possible literary larceny, since he is of course out of copyright.

Then and now, I would sometimes have to mug up the politicians of Queen Anne and the Hanoverian succession, to make sense of Swift's targets. Then and now, I would sometimes wonder if Swift thought them worth his talents. Did he think, why am I toiling to compose matchless prose to make these people immortal? Did he sometimes cast aside his quill, shout "Godolphin[58] is a swillbelly[59]" and slope off to the Brothers' Club for a little gargle with Bolingbroke[60] and his mates?

If Swift were alive today, he would have felt that way about the present ministry. He would simply use the epithet software on his laptop to call Dominic Cummings a pilgarlic[61] or Michael Gove an arsworm[62] and then have a steamy Zoom session with Stella.

---

[58] Leading minister under Queen Anne, backed and financed Marlborough.
[59] Seventeenth century slang for a big drinker.
[60] Tory statesman and political philosopher. Patron of Swift under Queen Anne. Fled England at Hanoverian succession and backed (losing) Stuart Pretender.
[61] A bald man (derogatory)
[62] A small man (derogatory)

Swift would never have sent Boris Johnson to Lilliput because it would imply that there was something to diminish.

Trump is something else. Terrible but not trivial, and a proper target for time-travelling Swift. But it is monumentally hard to satirize Trump when he does such a brilliant job of doing it himself. Trump's behaviour is calculated. He does not mind how many people think he is a monster so long as they also think he is a giant, and so long as enough of them hate his enemies more than they hate him. One has to find a way to mock Trump without actually helping him. That task might even defeat the genius of Jonathan Swift. With a final despairing cry of "Trump is a slubberdegullion"[63] he might give up and compose some additional Remarks on the Barrier Treaty.[64]

---

[63] A worthless scoundrel
[64] 1712 work by Swift attacking England's Dutch allies.

29 May

"The world's great age begins anew The golden years return."

Mandelson the Mystery Virus has left. And a source tells me...

Prodnose: Just a source?

Myself: Thank you. For once your intrusion had value. Sudden joie de vivre had led me to forget the iron laws of cliché. I should of course have said, a well-placed source. A curious term has entered American journalism: sources who know about the matter. It is sadly necessary these days to distinguish them from sources who know nothing about the matter, who are cited frequently, especially by Donald Trump. To resume, a well-placed source who knows about the matter told me that the human counterpart to Mandelson the Virus has as much chance of becoming the next Director-

General of the World Trade Organization as I have of winning the final of Strictly Come Dancing Down The Wicket.

"The Earth doth like a snake renew Her winter weeds outworn." The day got better. A new contact lens arrived, replacing the one which escaped to the Swiss frontier. I found an old polishing cloth which restored the silver bibelots to their original Georgian brilliance. Unfortunately the George in question was the Sixth.

And better yet... The Resident Mouse has Writer's Block. It is cruel to gloat. (Roars for several minutes). I could tell instantly. He was pacing so furiously as to drown out the fornicating foxes. I am surprised it did not happen earlier. After so many days composing his kind of uplifting glup, one's senses simply shut down. They know this in the Christmas card industry, where, at set intervals, production operatives are removed to a darkened room with readings of Dostoevski (Dusty to his rare friends). The little chap should be honoured to join the fraternity of Blocked Writers. In spite of his huge output, Dickens was a member. You can always tell when he was blocked approaching his deadlines. Suddenly there will be a long description of London in the fog, or some minor forgotten character will make a comeback. They show up like the joins in Prodnose's evening wig. At salon soirées, the poor sap thinks people are laughing at his jests.

"Heaven smiles and faiths and empires gleam Like wrecks of a dissolving dream."

And better yet… I attended an outdoor cricket net for the first time since lockdown. I was uncertain of its legality so I had prepared my Cummings defence. "Officer, I feared that I might have developed the yips.[65] I therefore travelled to this net to establish whether I was fit to bowl." I bowled. And no sign of the yips at all as I purveyed the familiar mixture of zombie, zamboni, zooter, zorker

---

[65] A sudden total loss of control which affects golfers and tennis-players as well as bowlers at cricket

(continues page 948723). Obediently the leather traveller assumed the required trajectories. Indeed, the zamboni, often a troublesome customer, came out as easily as the rest. I even found a new way to deliver the zzzombie, the ultra-slow version which often induces sleep in its recipients.

The usual crowd of local batters lined up to ~~enjoy the feast,~~ (corrects) test their skills, but social distancing rules required me to ration them. And world must have leaked out to my wider public, as encouraging messages poured in from former opponents, especially in Pakistan. "Don't give up … You've still got something to offer…."

30 May

My right shoulder has always had to do a lot of work when I bowl the zombie, the zamboni (continues Volume 94) because my arm whirls around twice. Indeed, the right shoulder can claim to be 144 years old compared to the more normal left one, which is still only 72. The right shoulder has never been more painful, but it was not from delivering the zombie etc. I blame the housework. Because of the COVID virus, it has to be done, er, properly compared to normal conditions. The Mouse can no longer achieve the required depth of cleaning, and in any event he has returned to writing his soppy volume <u>Keep Squeaking Through.</u>

I cured his Writer's Block in my sleep. Relieved of Mandelson the Mystery Virus, my dreams apparently resumed their normal supply of bromides and he helped himself to three more.

If you must have a deadly sin, choose sloth. Then you won't bother with the other six.

When you're in a slump, it's just life taking the chance of a little nap.

The universe is trying to send you a big package of joy, but if you're not in it will be left with a neighbour.

In case Mandelson returns when the Mouse is blocked again, I left him my two personal remedies. He studied the first and looked puzzled.

"My selection from the works of James Pye", I explained. "Against some fierce competition from Alfred Austin he won the title of England's worst-ever Poet Laureate, appointed in 1790 for his political reliability. In fairness to poor old Pye he wrote some worthwhile Shakespearean criticism and a thoughtful manual on the duties of Justices of the Peace. Here is Pye's effort on the birth of the future George IV.

Come happy child! Delight the land
Where time shall fix thy throne.
O come and take from Freedom's hand
A sceptre all her own
And when the sacred love of truth

Displayed shall form thy ripening youth,
May every joyful BRITON find
The soul of GEORGE's godlike race
With lovely CHARLOTTE's softer grace
Attempered on thy mind…"

"There's more?" said the Mouse. What there is of his mouth was wide open.

"Much more, but now have a look at this". I handed him the reviews of Prodnose's only novel, which he rashly titled Modern Life, and was intended to establish him as a latter-day Zola. "A more accurate choice would have been Gorgonzola", I added and the Mouse gave me a few of his characteristic squoars.

He read though the cuttings. The critics could not decide which was worse, the plot, the characters, the dialogue or the style, although one was deceived into thinking it a satirical masterpiece. "An astonishing debut. Reginald Prodnose remorselessly dissects the endless banality of modern life. His novel is a wicked montage of nonentity babbling to nonentity."

"Why have you made me read all this?" asked my companion, by now even ashener than when listening to my Mandelson narrative some days ago.

"To tell you that Writers Block is given to those of us with something to say. It is nature's way of telling us to pause and let our thoughts and words mature like a vat of fine old Glen Close single-malt whisky ("the attraction is fatal"). Writers Block tells you that you are not a Pye or a Prodnose. Think how much literature would have gained if only they had been blocked instead."

This was distinctly flattering to the rodent author of <u>Keep Squeaking Through</u> but I knew that he had had a bad shock. My remedy worked. He started to puff out his chest, insofar as a mouse has a chest to puff.

In case you are wondering, Prodnose's actual novel is available only on prescription, for cases of impedimentum literarium extremum.

31 May

The Mouse has company. This message was waiting on the computer when I woke from a light but unMandelblighted sleep.

hey boss i hope you don't mind my coming back and staying for a bit because all this hygiene stuff aint too good for us cockroaches and i thought maybe at your place it aint so much of an issue sorry i guess i couldve put that better still no hard feelings i hope for your old pal archy ps you were shouting some crazy upbeat stuff in your sleep i thought any minute you were going to sing kumbaya is everything ok a

"Archy!" I exclaimed. "Pardon me, archy. Why are you still in lower case? I taught you how to work the shift key."

my public expect it

Can't argue with that. He's been in the literary business longer than I have.

"Welcome back, archy. I've had to raise the hygiene game too, but you can stay for as long as you like. Just avoid the neighbours, they might get the wrong impression of you."

"Who's staying?" It was the Mouse and he asked it in a marked manner. I introduced them, discovering for the first time that the Mouse's name was Mortimer. I didn't have the heart to tell him about the Mortimer Mouse who failed as a movie actor until his agent persuaded him to change his name to Mickey. Mortimer hardly listened to my account of archy's career and his awardwinning nine-volume life of mehitabel the cat. He said "Can I have a word with you please?" for all the world like Eric Morecombe to Ernie Wise[66] about an awkward guest star. We moved in the direction of aside.

"I don't want to hear any cat story," said Mortimer. "He stays off my cheese board. No visitors after 9pm. And I want first dibs on your dreams." He stalked away still in an obvious snit.

(Sighs deeply.) Has it come to this? After nearly sixty years service to the republic of letters I must now shuttle like Henry Kissinger between a rodent and an insect.

In the event archy had no problem with any of the terms.

---

[66] Hugely popular British comedy duo whose television show regularly saw them conspire against some major guest star.

look boss whoever heard of a cockroach who liked
cheese and he can keep all that sappy dream stuff
of yours ive gone into the haiku game i dont know
why i didnt try it before all you gotta do is count to
17 and folks will take anything

"I think there's more to it, archy". (I find it relaxing
sometimes to deliver the feed line instead of the
zinger.)

nuts listen here's one supposed to be a classic

in my hut this spring
there is nothing
there is everything

i know it loses a lot in the original tell you one
thing though those old japanese poets didnt have a
problem with insects they keep writing about them

they make a cockroach
live better in a haiku
than any hotel

Sap from Mortimer, pap from archy... All I need now is for the foxes to land a publishing deal.

<u>1 June</u>

I shall never live down the shame if I have been duped by a fake roach.

And it's something I should have spotted right away from his message. Something spotted at once by my concerned friend Lou Burnard. Why, after more than a century of communicating only in free verse, should alleged-archy write to me in continuous prose?

I'm a live-and-let-live kind of guy. Correction. I'm a serious coward. But I have my responsibilities to world literature. I knew I must challenge alleged-archy to protect the real one's reputation and possibly also his royalties. I fortified myself for the ordeal with some deep draughts of very old Glen Hoddle single-malt whisky ("try it in long passes"). I confronted the roach and put the question to him right away to give him no time to think of a politician's answer.

He narrowed his five eyes and roughly 10,000 lenses. (What happens when a cockroach needs glasses?) No pins dropped, cats and dogs stopped yapping, foxes stopped fornicating and I could hear a deafening racket from butterflies flapping their wings in what's left of the Amazon. He opened them all again and said

in hard times like these
one learns the art of begging
prose as well as verse

It was plausible. It was also a haiku, confirming the roach's recent claim. But I needed much more evidence. I fired questions at him. He knew all the details of mehitabel's life and his long experience as

Don Marquis's lodger. But these have a large following and would be readily available to a determined impostor. So I moved on to episodes from his interlude with me three years ago, known only to the real archy and the handful of connoisseurs who followed my account of them.

"What was the first food I offered you?"

a ferrero roacher chocolate you swiped from some ambassador

"Which of my songs did you enjoy in performance?"

ping the pong ball of my heart, dear

"Who then tried to injunct any future performance?"

all your neighbours (gives a roachy roar)
no actually it was a lawyer called denali from the firm of gumby pokey and prickle

Then the roach revealed a fact which had never been published. (Waits.) I said, a fact which had never been published.

Mortimer Mouse: Oh sorry. You mean?...

Myself: That's right, Mortimer. Only the real archy could have known.

Mortimer Mouse: But maybe you blurted it in your sleep. You didn't give me anything last night for my book whose title I will just mention casually at dictation speed: Keep… Squeaking… Through. The roach cut in. All his eyes and lenses darted around the room. Even with the newly polished bibelots it had crossed the frontier from lived-in to dingy.

listen boss
no offence i hope
but if i went to all this trouble
to be a fake archy
wouldnt i try to live
in better premises

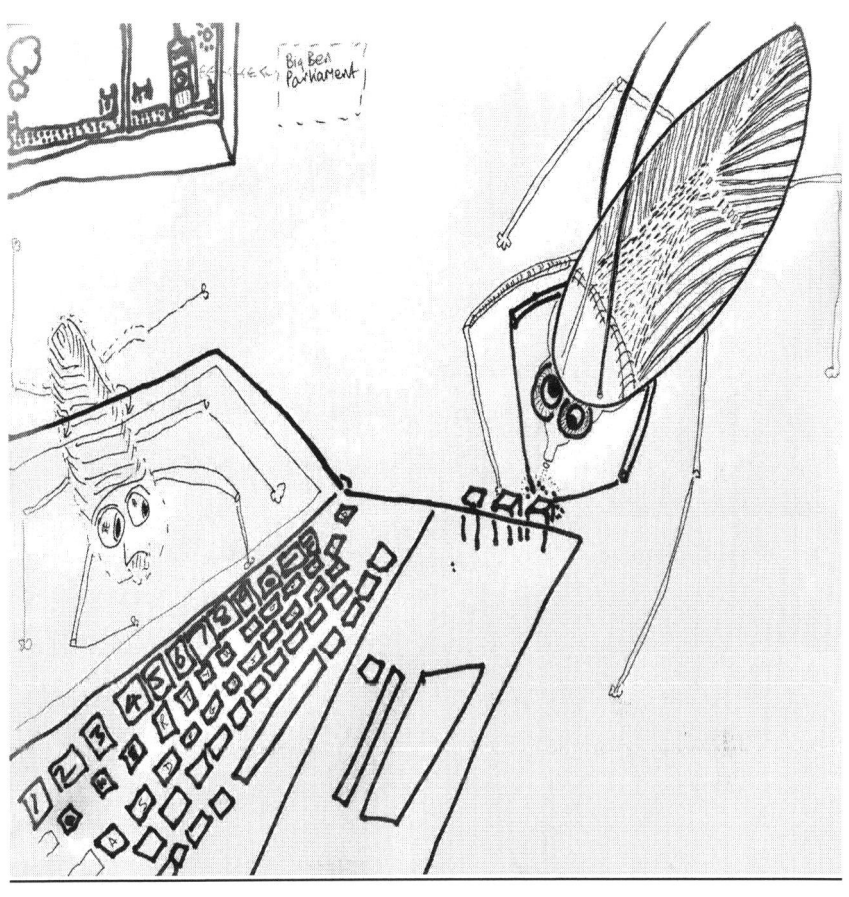

A fake roach?

<u>2 June</u>

I still have my doubts about my new lodger. I am going to call him kidding-artist-formerly-known-as-archy or kafkaa, calling to mind the creator of another troublesome insect.

kafkaa is now on good terms with Mortimer Mouse. He has actually given him lessons in artistic temperament. I can now do nothing which interferes with their creation of drivelling haikus or soggy soundbites. In my own residence I have become a servant and a prisoner of a roach and a rodent. Mortimer, under kafkaa's influence, has even started to demand better aphorisms from my dreams.

The two have severely limited my repertoire on the piano. Mortimer will listen only to "Pick Yourself Up." I have become sick to death of Jerome Kern's opening chords: plunk-plunka-plunka-plunka. Even the major 7ths. And I love major 7ths. They are the fresh lime juice of music. I stick lots of major 7ths into songs when the composer has foolishly forgotten to use them. As for kafkaa, he insists on ping the pong ball of my heart dear, archy's favourite on his previous visit. But I think kafkaa is faking it, and simply mouthing my lyrics to my accompaniment. In fairness, it is hard to detect whether a cockroach is mouthing, and many human singers have been known to mouth when I accompany them. Or even mouth off.

The neighbours cannot understand why I am playing the same two numbers over and over again. In these hygienic times, I cannot reveal that I am harbouring a cockroach and a mouse, never mind performing for them and accommodating their every caprice. I mumble something about mastering a new modulation.

Of course it has become impossible to continue in these conditions my own memoirs, <u>My Goodness How I Roared!</u> Is it fair to literature to sacrifice myself in this way? It is as if... as if... Alexander Pope had made himself an unpaid housekeeper to slashing Bentley or piddling Tibbalds, dismal denizens of his <u>Dunciad.</u>

Here are Mortimer's latest pensées (unassisted by my sleep).

When it's too dark to see, you could try removing your sunglasses.

When you need a helping hand, walk south from your elbow.

When life is a frost, make a snowman.

And kafkaa's latest haiku.

the gap has been filled
the void has been replenished
by a new abyss

I could not help sniggering.

whats the big joke

"I remembered an English exam question from my school days, correcting this sentence: 'At the end of the twisting mountain path was an awful yawning abbess.'"

MGHIR! not that I did at the time.

Mortimer Mouse rushed in, all breathless. "This… just… in…" he gasped, "From Fox News."

"And you believe it?"

"I mean the ones outside. They've just been signed to make a porn video on outdoor sex. They're setting up the lights just below our window."

Before I could push back on his use of "our window" he added "And that's not all. The director's a descendant of Charlie Chaplin."

"You mean?..." I could spot my cue.

"That's right, Richard", said Mortimer in triumph. "He's a perfectionist. He could ask for 342 takes. With screeches in each one."

I felt like a drowning camel from whom the last straw had been removed.

Prodnose: But surely a drowning camel would welcome the removal of a straw? Or had he woven the straw into some form of primitive lifejacket? Please explain....

3 June

a roach writes

richard is away
preparing his new podcast
for all cricket fans

he has to pretend
to have read all the novels
featuring cricket

knowing him i think
he might pretend he really
wrote them all himself

roachy roars

would listen to him
if id become a cricket
and not a cockroach

<u>4 June</u> (nothing glorious about it this year)

Could Donald Trump be an agent sent by Satan to try to turn people against God? Asking on behalf of a friend.

Many people now ask "What would Jesus have done?" But it is equally important to ask "What would Satan have done in the name of Jesus?" It's amazing how often Donald Trump supplies the answer.

I am worried that the Trump gang intercepted my revised script for <u>Seven Days In May,</u> about a successful military coup in the United States, which I sent to the Chairman of the Joint Chiefs of Staff, General Mark A Milley (see 25 May). The general was pictured in combat gear supporting Trump's recent Washington photo-op. I believe this person was an imposter. The Trump gang are running an imposter for Nadia, the poor sick tiger at the Bronx Zoo (see earlier), so they would not have any scruples about impersonating a four-star general. The real General Milley, Marky-Mark to his friends, is an educated soldier, who knows that it would be catastrophic to involve America's armed forces to support a racially-motivated violent re-election bid by any American President, let alone one who needs to rely on voter suppression. (This is the big story of the current election and as usual, it is being ignored.) He would not willingly have joined Trump's walkabout in such a costume, and I think the Trump gang have him locked away somewhere. I can tweak the script to include his daring escape, but I wish actors would not interfere with my work.

On the other hand, perhaps it was the real general, and Trump deceived him about the photo-op, like the Defense Secretary, a Mr Esper, who also appeared. Trump told him they were going out for ice cream. Did he tell the general it was a rehearsal for trick-or-treating?

It might simply be that Trump is a tool used by Vladimir Putin to destroy the United States. But could Vladimir Putin be an agent sent by Satan to try to turn people against God's Russian Orthodox branch?

5 June

Johnny Virus does not know or care whether you are protesting in a good cause: it is dangerous and anti-social to hold any kind of mass demonstration in these times. Indeed, if Johnny Virus has any political agenda he is a reactionary and a racist, since he is more likely to kill poor people than rich, and (apparently) BAME people rather than white. Why help him?

So here's an alternative form of protest which could be done massively but also distantly. For alliterative reasons alone I'll focus it on Trump and call it the Donald Dirge.

At a given moment, people would play, sing, or chant one chosen minor chord – against Trump. E Flat Minor should be in most people's range. They could play it together (the biggest loudest chord ever played) or in relay as people pick up the chord from each other, making the longest chord in history. Famous performers in all musical genres might lead this event.

Originally I thought this might take place when Trump is formally renominated on August 27. But that now seems too late, and we should make an earlier musical Date with Donald (didn't want to call it D-Day, which should be reserved for those remembered tomorrow.) At twelve noon on the chosen Date, people would perform the Donald Dirge. If this were a global event, the Donald Dirge could be passed from east to west to hit twelve noon in each time zone. If successful, it could become the Daily Donald Dirge.

Of course there might be some musical retaliation from Trump supporters. But I have to believe that in a contest among the world's musicians Trump would go down to a landslide defeat.

This form of protest need not and should not be confined to Trump. Putin should get a dirge too in a different key, and conventional Western tuning would allow for ten other tyrannical targets. There might be more appropriate local musical dirges for Mr Hsi, the Paramount Brute in China, and the Crown Prince of Saudi Arabia.

It would be too flattering to allot a musical chord to Boris Johnson. A mass issue of kazoos is quite enough for him.

<u>6 June</u>

The foxes shot their porn video outside my window for the perfectionist descendant of Charlie Chaplin. Or so I'm told by Mortimer Mouse and kafkaa the cockroach. The director was apparently even noisier than the foxes with his screams for cuts and retakes.

kafkaa showed me a haiku about the proceedings.

the foxes screeched all night
but none of their ecstasy
gave satisfaction

Mortimer tried to get some uplift from them: when you can't sleep, just think of it as life's added time for injuries and stoppages. But there was no pep in his work. His whiskers were drooping faster than Boris Johnson's ratings.

But I did not hear the foxes or their director. I lay awake all night thinking of Donald Trump. Score one to the Commander-in-chief. He would probably claim to be dominating my battlespace, although he is not a great authority on battlespace because of those awful bonespurs detected by his podiatrist which frustrated his efforts to serve in Vietnam. It is inspiring that he overcame them to become such a great golfer.

Mortimer, who seems to have an inside track on these matters, says that the director liked none of the rushes and wants to re-shoot all the porno fox footage again tonight. The normally stoic kafkaa is moved to raise all five of his eyebrows, but the news leaves me cold. I will be spending another night with Donald Trump.

If it resulted in the removal of Donald Trump I would abandon cricket, piano-playing and all literary output. I would give up fresh lime juice and turn my plantation in São Tomé e Príncipe into a sanctuary for the endangered pangolin. I would not just wash but massage the feet of beggars. I would spend the rest of my life with Mandelson the Mystery Virus without the aid of very old Glen Gould Canadian single-malt whisky ("make your own music"). Is Anyone Up There listening?

7 June

Mortimer Mouse is the hero of the hour. A sentence rarely written, and I hope he will savour it over his selection from the cheese counter at Fortnum & Mason which I have just ordered for him.

He secured a night of peace from the screeching foxes and their even louder director. He persuaded them to employ him as their agent. He told them that their talents were underpriced and badly showcased in the porn video they were making at Rubato Towers. They deserved a far more opulent setting than "this crumbling pile". I looked momentarily askance at this description, which brought a snigger from kafkaa (I have learnt to distinguish this from his full-throated roachy roars).

"Do not look so askance," said Mortimer, who is getting quite acute in noticing such things. "Feeding their ego was my lone weapon." His stratagem certainly worked. The foxes are now holding out for Lord's cricket ground as a location, since no one else is using it until further notice, and they want the actual square not the Nursery ground. Mortimer also persuaded them to fire the director and demand the legendary "Whispering One-take" Will Wrappit.

I still could not sleep because of Donald Trump. But the least I could do for Mortimer was to set aside my memoirs (again) and spend the day devising new sugar drops for his uplifting volume <u>Keep Squeaking Through.</u>

When life has you on your knees, plant a few crocuses while you're down there.

Somewhere in the world, at any moment, there's a very fat man in a top hat stepping on a banana skin.

Congratulations! You have been chosen for the remake of It's A Wonderful Life.

Even with my conscious or unconscious help, I don't think Mortimer is going to finish his book. He is caught up in his new role and scurries about Rubato Towers babbling phrases he thinks movie agents use. "Have your people talk to my people… my client's name goes on the left…." and one he might have picked up from my experience, "no unsolicited submissions."

8 June

Mortimer Mouse is the villain of the hour. I have cancelled his Fortnum & Mason cheeses.

Mind you, I should have known what would happen when he persuaded the foxes to behave like movie stars. Exactly like Cymbeline, Shakespeare's performing bear, all those years ago, they each acquired their own entourage. Personal trainers, personal chefs, personal brush stylists, personal dialogue coaches (as if they need a dialogue coach for "Screech! Screech!"), personal flea removers, and, some way below the flea removers, personal writers. And what does an entourage do? Whatever the star does. So when the two Fox Stars began a… a… (holds down cliché button) … a steamy sex romp the two entourages held steamy sex romps of their own. With screeches of their own. All in different keys.

It was so loud and discordant that I even stopped thinking about Donald Trump. The pain was so terrible that kafkaa begged me to Do Something in upper case. We both looked at Mortimer in a marked manner. Nothing was said (it would have been futile anyway in the racket) but he could not look into kafkaa's implacable fourth eye. Finally, the Stars stopped and the entourages stopped instantly and obediently as entourages should. The Stars lounged on the roof of the rich neighbour's Porsche and the entourages draped themselves over the moss-encrusted jalopies abandoned by the neighbours who moved away. Oddly enough, they were the ones right underneath my piano, the ones who kept banging on the ceiling for encores. I hope they found another pianist near their new place.

I hit the cliché button again. "Hurry, there's no time to lose", I told Mortimer and kafkaa, and under my directions they ran extension speakers from my keyboard to the foxes' romping ground outside my window. kafkaa was not up to the heavy lifting but he was an absolute whizz at connecting the funny-shaped thingummy into the whatever. When all the foxes returned after their little rest, I was ready for them. At the first screech I began to play, rubatissimo, pah-lunk-plunk-plunk pah-lunk-plunk-plunk pah-lunk-plunk-plunk-plunk-plunk and then kafkaa and Mortimer joined me in a mighty chorus: "Foxey, foxey, you know you're a cute little heart breaker, ha, Foxey yeah and you know you're a sweet little love maker, ha Foxey."

For a second the foxes were stilled. Then they were all at it worse than ever. You would have thought they were plankton. Sex, sex, sex, that's all plankton ever think about. Not that they think much. "Thick as two short plankton." That's what all my mollusc friends say.

"Fool!" I said to myself.

"Fool!" said Mortimer to me.

"FOOL" said kafkaa, enraged into full upper case although an exclamation mark was still beyond him.

I had made quite the wrong musical selection. My rubatissimo made little difference to the Jimi Hendrix masterpiece. All the foxes actually appeared to enjoy it. I switched instantly to a number which needed strict timing, the charming 1930s number "How Am I Gonna Keep The News From Mother?" A fox trot. Made popular by Roy Fox and his orchestra.

The romping mob outside endured a few bars. Then with a final screech, in which I detected pain rather than ecstasy, the Fox Stars broke and ran. Obediently the entourages broke and ran with them. Rubato Towers enjoyed a sudden peace, broken only by the sound of the neighbours' goldfish bridge party when West, the Rueful Rookie Ryukin, accidentally revoked.

Mortimer Mouse was fired (by telegram) as the Fox Stars' agent and has resumed his old life as a writing drudge. I told him my two agent jokes as a punishment, you know, the one about the heart transplant and the one about the sharks. MGHIR! extra hard.

9 June

As if I have not enough creatures in my life, the neighbour has asked me to give a few bridge tutorials to Rufus the Rueful Rookie Ryukin. Never a confident performer, his nerve is completely shot after he revoked and presented an unmakeable slam to the experienced partnership of Sheldon and Sheila the Sharp Shubunkins. His partner, Culbert the Comet, totted up the score very slowly with a series of carping remarks. I said, carping… fish… carping… Again, MGHIR!

My neighbour likes to impress. There are now many places which offer tropical fish for visitors to admire, but few allow them at the same time to be kibitzers at a marine rubber of bridge. To get his finny friends into the mood, my neighbour serves them flakes in the shapes of clubs, diamonds, hearts and spades.

Prodnose: This is getting ridiculous even for you. Goldfish cannot play bridge. They cannot remember any card longer than seven seconds. (Cackles)

Myself (with a thin smile as momentary as Melania Trump's): The seven-second memory is a bit of fake news put out by goldfish themselves to allow them to ignore things they do not wish to retain, such as your prose. Goldfish are actually expert card counters. Have you ever seen any goldfish at the blackjack table of any major casino?

Prodnose: Of course not!

Myself: Exactly. They've all been banned. The only problem for goldfish with bridge is to sort and fan a hand of thirteen cards. They overcome this by having all the hands shuffled and dealt electronically and then displayed on the walls of the bridgequarium, which is of course divided into four watertight compartments. Each fish bids and plays his or her hand by tapping the buttons on a tiny panel. They are rather close together and beginners such as poor Rufus often revoke until they get used to them.

Prodnose: And I suppose you'll turn Rufus the Rueful Rookie Ryukin into Omar Sharif? (Snorts).

Myself (neutrally): That may be beyond my powers. But if he listens to me I will make him unbeatable in post-deal analysis, which matters in bridge far more than any actual wins or losses. "Let's see what happens if you ruff my eight of spades with the six and partner then under-ruffs with the five asking me for a diamond when I get back in…." That kind of thing. I don't know how long it will take to get Rufus to that level and now

I've got to teach a bridge convention to every American voter.

Prodnose (obligingly): And what's that?

Myself: A Strong No-Trump. My goodness, how I'd roar if it weren't so serious.

<u>10 June</u>

A Goldfish Writes: Was my face red! I'd played the wrong card and let my partner down. I thought I would give up bridge and play parcheesi for the rest of my life. But Richard Heller gave me a few lessons – and now I can play any card I like and give my partner the perfect reason for it. Remember the name. Richard Heller. Don't lose heart, he's a diamond geezer, he'll make you a welcome fourth in any club, and his modest fee get spade back many times over (gets paid back, geddit???)

Myself: Most gratifying. One takes any unsolicited testimonial at this stage of indigent obscurity and the gurgled gratitude of a goldfish is as welcome as the tap on the shoulder from the Nobel Committee. Well, actually no, it isn't. That's a bridge too far. But thank you, anyway, Rufus. It was a joy to see you so confidently ignoring your partner's request for a spade lead and then rattling off my explanation that you'd thought he was attempting a reverse peter, or retep, as we experts call them, asking for any heart lower than the five. At no extra charge I taught Rufus my favourite You-Play-It Partner convention, the one where you induce partner to bid No-Trumps early on and then "save" in it at the highest possible level. This nearly always allows you to tot up the penalty points in silent reproach, and it is worth paying the very occasional price of an unendurable partner bringing home an "impossible" contract.

When facing serious embarrassment at the bridge table, I resort to my old stratagem of pretending to lose a contact lens (see much earlier). This is not much use to goldfish although I did once see a Celestial Eye affecting a set of pince-nez.

And now the other neighbour wants me to teach his cockatiel my variations of the Ruy Lopez, which helped Bobby Fischer prepare for his famous battle in Reykjavik against Spassky the Commie chess champion. Work, work, work!

<u>11 June</u>

Prodnose: You claim to have worked on the Ruy Lopez with Bobby Fischer before his great match with Boris Spassky?

Myself (waking from feverish sleep): Hmm? Oh, it's you. Indeed.

Prodnose: Then how do you explain that Bobby Fischer only twice played the Ruy Lopez?

Myself (pityingly): I told him to avoid it. Of course, Bobby was a law unto himself. But you will of course remember 26 Bb3! in game 10?

Prodnose (obligingly): You mean?...

Myself (giving a thin smile of satisfaction before resubsiding into fevered sleep).

(Later)

a cockroach writes:

richard is unwell
but not like jeffrey bernard
mandelson again

A Goldfish writes:

This bout looks like a real slam and Richard may be dummy for some time.

A Mouse writes:

I will continue to monitor his dreams for his public and mine. Meanwhile, you may like to know that a stuck glass stopper may be loosened with a few drops of olive oil around the stopper and bottle neck. Warm the bottle gently and tap the stopper with a wooden spoon.

12 June

Johnny Virus still stalks our country and the world, killing people at will, especially if they are poor or BAME. To these victims can be added all those still being killed in the ordinary way through other diseases or persecution, displacement, deprivation and wars. The Earth is still being trashed and raped. The United States is in the hands of a demented proto-dictator (with an imitation in Brazil), China, Russia and our dear ally Saudi Arabia are ruled by tyrants on the basis of lies, corruption and violence. Democracy is fragile or dead in dozens of other countries. Our own country is ruled by a glib, lazy dolt.

Against this background, it is heartening that so many progressives still have the time and energy to campaign about memorials to long-dead people, and there will be global rejoicing at their victories. There will be a poster before very long in which two politically-advanced children confront a shamed parent with the question: "What did you do in the Great Statue War, Daddy?"

It might be helpful for everyone to remember that like Lord Melbourne's Order of the Garter there's no demm'd merit in being a statue. London statues are a random collection of worthies and wasters. Whitehall, for example, is dominated by two of Britain's worst soldiers. The whiskered Duke of Cambridge was a Royal clot, whom even his cousin, Queen Victoria, called "poor George." His main contribution as Commander-in-Chief of the British Army was to oppose any essential army reform. Worse still, Earl Haig stares at the Cenotaph commemorating so many men whom he sent uselessly to their deaths. (Yes, I know Haig's is a fine statue and he's had a bit of a comeback historically.) Gazing at Cambridge and Haig from a siding in Whitehall are two of Britain's greatest soldiers, Slim and Alan Brooke.

If any statue has really become unbearable for the present generation, rather than vandalize it or tear it from its moorings, it would be far cheaper to scatter it with pigeon food and let our feathered friends express our feelings for us.

Meanwhile, we all might usefully and creatively prepare a list of subjects who deserve a statue but haven't got one. I suggested that the slaver Robert Milligan might be replaced by his distant relative Spike, and was delighted to learn that there is a Spike statue in Finchley. What about Peter Sellers? I know he was born in Southsea but he did wonderful work in London. Or is he out of court for his "regressive" portrayal of a trade unionist in I'm All Right Jack? How about Nijinsky (the horse would win a ballot over the dancer)? Or Winnie-the-Pooh and friends to match Paddington Bear (we foolishly lost the original toys to the New York Public Library)?

Any new statues, even children's favourites, had best be mounted on castors, so that they can be removed in a hurry when they offend generations unknown.

13 June

Mandelson the Mystery Virus is a master of fake remissions. He appears to disappear…

Prodnose: Did you mean that?

Myself: Oxy – MORON! But then he comes back, as malign as before. But after all, that's why I named it Mandelson. (Plays "I'll be seeing you, in all the old familiar places." Subsides, narrowly missing the still dodgy F sharp over middle C). I will not weary my public with the old familiar symptoms. He does make me forget the Great Statue War. He even makes me forget Donald Trump and all the other terrible people and things mentioned yesterday. But I would still rather be awake than asleep all day.

A Goldfish Writes: That sounds like a real Yarborough.

a cockroach writes:

does this alone last
from here to eternity
peter mandelson

A Mouse Writes: Life sends us Brussels sprouts so that we can enjoy the ice cream afterwards.

Even on Pluto you can see the Sun. So get your deckchair out!

No lockdown is as lasting as a closed mind. (Snatched from Richard's dreams.)

14 June

With so many important statues still unsmashed, I admit it is selfish to rail against Mandelson, my Mystery Virus.

Prodnose: Good heavens, do you support statue-smashing?

Myself: You back again? Had I known I would have inserted a bracketed {Irony Alert} or even made that crass gesture with doubled fingers to represent "….". (Turns face to wall.) Why can a fake roach, a Panglossian mouse and a card-crazed goldfish recognize irony but not he, a supposed ambassador of the republic of letters? My faithful public, you and I are keepers of a sputtering flame. Prodnoses rule a post-ironic world, where, as if under the compulsion of some terrifying literary Health and Safety Inspectorate, irony cannot be used unless it is labelled IRONY and displays all its contents.

I was about to complain (without irony or subtext of any kind) that Mandelson plunges me regularly into a drab semi-life neither asleep nor awake, neither thinking nor dreaming…

Mortimer Mouse: You gave me three absolute zingers when you did drop off.

Myself (reluctantly curious): Reveal, rodent!

Mortimer Mouse: A man slips on a banana skin. He falls and curses. But if he had missed it and turned the corner, he would have been hit by a skidding truck.

Your past is nothing more than the first rushes of an unfinished movie. Edit it and insist on director's cut.

Somewhere in this world, at any time, a nightingale sings to an elephant in a stream and a child is reunited with a lost puppy.

Myself: You shock me again. I had no idea that my subconscious was such an ocean of mush.

Prodnose (spitefully): You're no ironist. All your novels are ridiculously sentimental. And I've seen you blubbing every time you re-read one.

Myself: That was for their sales, not their content.

<u>15 June</u>

On masked forays into London's public transport, I have frequently noticed a poster with a bizarre, cryptic slogan: Vote With Your Buttocks. I think this is a trial for a new campaign to re-elect Boris Johnson.

Prodnose (sniffily): That sounded a bit cheap.

Myself (snarls): Not for that feckless fustian fleabrained foul fiend Flippertegibbet. (Feeling better.) Shops reopen today, a chance for us all to reacquaint ourselves with merchandise we were glad to do without. However, I will nip out and buy the Eritrean curtains which were capriciously denied to me on April 13.

All shops will be compelled to enforce social distancing, a forlorn hope with the crazed mobs satisfying their pent-up demand for fridge magnets. At least there will be no tourists fighting each other over displays of snowglobes and teddy bears dressed as Beefeaters.

I foresee major problems with the prohibition against trying on clothes. Thousands of people of all genders and some we haven't yet thought of will buy clothes in the size they think they are rather than the one they really are. When they try them on at home, they will quail at the toil and embarrassment of returning to the shop to exchange them. Some vain shoppers will cram as much of themselves as will fit into these clothes, but others may provide a bonanza for such charity shops as have survived lockdown.

Bookshops will be compelled to quarantine any volumes which have been browsed but not purchased. This could generate a new sanction against authors. J K Rowling (Jekyll to her special friends) may become a victim, since she seems to have offended a great many people for reasons I have not quite understood. Her opponents could organize a mass browsing of all her works and secure their withdrawal from open display in bookshops.

Happily, this sanction will never be applied to mine.

16 June

Britain's zoos have reopened but subject to social distancing rules. I hope that they have told all the inmates and trained them to stay two metres apart. Some species are notoriously bad listeners. Yes, zebras, I'm looking at you. Reptile houses are to remain shut. That might still be a necessary precaution against Johnny Virus, but that's not how the snakes will see it. To them, it will just seem like another episode in the long history of herpetophobia since the book of Genesis.

In America, the Bronx Zoo, where Nadia the tiger caught the virus, remains shut. I never had a reply to the questions I sent to her (see earlier), which only confirms my theory that poor Nadia perished and is being impersonated by a replacement tiger. Her handlers obviously need more time to coach her, but I have one question for which no amount of coaching could prepare her.

I admit that I was a little shaken by Prodnose's charge two days ago that all my novels are ridiculously sentimental. I re-read them all (it didn't take long) and by gum, they are very sentimental, but the fool did not recognize that they are sentimental in a witty, self-mocking post-modern way, as were the new tears with which I drenched the clever, knowing happy endings. Besides, what's wrong with tears? One of my favourite books is T H White's eclectic history of the eighteenth century <u>The Age Of Scandal.</u> It has a whole chapter on tears. The century was full of them and rejoiced in their open display, red-blooded men who gambled immense sums and fought duels as much as any. It was Victorian public schools who introduced the cult of the stiff upper lip to stop boys complaining about the appalling food and conditions they had to endure. They left a long legacy of repressed emotion and words unsaid which was very useful to dramatists and trained generations of English actors to convey a lifetime of futile longing in the momentary flick of an eyebrow.

Prodnose: Redundant, surely? Are not eyebrow-flicks always momentary?

Myself: You never saw those of my late employer, Denis Healey. Anyway, the stiff upper lip mentality has crumbled under the assaults of generations X, Y and Z (what happens after Z?) Public emotion is fashionable again. I shall relaunch all my novels without their protective clingfilm of irony, as a guarantee of a really good cry.

17 June

My plans for a remake of Seven Days In May (see earlier), in which the Chairman of the Joint Chiefs of Staff, General "Marky-Mark" Milley, saves the country from an election stolen by Donald Trump, are in development hell.

Instead we are forced to contemplate this real-life scenario. After an election in which millions of likely Democrat voters are denied a vote, Trump nonetheless loses both in the popular vote and the Electoral College. However, he refuses to concede. By a mixture of legal challenges and outright intimidation, his supporters prevent the authorities in several key Democratic states from certifying their election returns. Joe Biden is thus denied the requisite majority in the Electoral College. The election is thrown to the House of Representatives, but not to the full (Democrat) House but to a delegation of one representative per state, regardless of population. A majority of these fifty people choose as President – Donald Trump.

The methods now being used to exclude likely Democrats (especially black, Hispanic, minority-ethnic, low-income, students, disabled people) from the ballot are so blatant as to have embarrassed Trump's friend and advisor, Vladimir Putin. (I made that up, but only a little.) The familiar method of denying them a convenient polling station, especially one adapted for disabled people, has become even more effective because of the virus. In state after state it is a long and expensive process for them to get a postal ballot instead – and if they do get one Trump has threatened to bankrupt the Post Office so that they cannot use it. Familiar identity documents, especially driving licenses, are suddenly made useless as identity for likely Democrats. They are being disqualified for felonies they never knew they had committed, and made to prove that they are not another person of the same name (or even sometimes a different name. I challenge any British voter to <u>prove</u> that he or she is not registered elsewhere as Lord Buckethead.) Korean-American voters have been asked to sign their names – in Korean, and disqualified if they make a mistake. If, in spite of all this, likely Democrats succeed in getting to a polling station with the expectation of being allowed to vote, they are likely to face Trump supporters mounting ad hoc challenges (on those who look easiest to intimidate.)

I have a proposal for any Americans who are unreasonably prevented from voting. I think it would be very popular, although unfortunately it would be too late to prevent a stolen election. They should withhold their income tax for the next four years. I have a slogan for this protest: no taxation without representation.

Prodnose (smugly): That's hardly original.

Myself (with an especially pitying smile): I was aware of that. But it is out of copyright. Tax rebellions are a hallowed American tradition, and this one might escalate into a second American revolution. Whole communities and counties might withhold their Federal tax from a cheating Chief Executive. Even whole states. Through the Federal budget, ten states (nearly all Democratic) subsidize the other forty. Some of these Blue Democratic states might say to the Red Republican ones: "OK, you gave us this asshole as President, you can pay for him."

In a second Trump administration based on force and fraud, public morality may collapse in the United States, as more and more Americans decide that they too will do things the Trump way: tell any lie they choose, break any law they choose, do down any other American they choose. If that happens, I will not drive a car in Trump's United States.

18 June

It's all but midsummer. There are no cricket matches being played in England, but Premier League football is restored (a product of science and common sense or money and supposed votes?) So too is Royal Ascot. Have they told the horses to observe social distancing? Any selections of mine have always done this without being asked, keeping a respectful two metres behind the rest of the field until compelled to accelerate by the runners in the next race.

The England and Wales Cricket Board has produced a road map for the return of recreational cricket matches. When any organization announces a road map one knows that it is totally adrift. One pictures all the cars becalmed on hard shoulders and verges, their drivers and passengers turning their road maps every which way in the baffled pursuit of their destination, or their modern equivalent, those losing all faith in the ignorant instructions from the hectoring voice of their satnav. I did not get where I am today by following a road map. Mind you, I have not got anywhere today, living in indigent obscurity with a sad salon of a rodent, a roach and a Ryukin.

While the ECB fiddles with its road map, hundreds of local clubs are haemorrhaging money for lack of match income, and more important, losing players permanently, especially young ones.

My good friend Wasim Akram did not dominate the world's batsmen by producing a road map towards toe-crushing late reverse swinging yorkers. He delivered them. If the ECB cared about club and recreational cricket it would have devised rules to allow cricket matches to be played within the guidelines for fighting Johnny Virus. It should not be difficult. Children's cricket has always had distancing provisions. Having devised these rules, it should present them to whichever drudge is Boris Johnson's Sports Minister…

Mortimer Mouse: It's Nigel Huddleston.

Myself: Well, fancy that! He'll be delighted to know that his fame has reached the mouseholes of Rubato Towers. I discover that he also does tourism (Britain's third biggest industry before Johnny Virus), heritage, civil society, whatever that is, and loneliness. Anyway, the ECB would tell Mr H that clubs would play cricket matches under its new rules unless the government forbids them.

If the ECB is too wet to do this, I shall have to take it over. As if I haven't got enough on my hands. Perhaps I could assign it to Mortimer. He knows the Sports Minister.

19 June

In tribute to Dame Vera Lynn[67], here is Eric Morecambe's inspired jest during the Falklands war: "I knew the situation was serious. I passed Vera Lynn's house and heard her gargling." My goodness, a whole nation roared!

My household at Rubato Towers was deeply affected by her passing. Under my tuition, Rufus the once-Rueful has become Rufus the Ruthless Ryukin in the bridgequarium. But when the news was brought to him, he solemnly declined to re-double for the first time in his career. Incidentally, it gets very confusing when bridge-playing amœbas decide to re-double.

kafkaa the cockroach claimed to have met Vera in a grimy dressing room during one of the many ENSA tours she made during the Second World War to inspire our forces.

---

[67] She died aged 103

what a great trouper
she did not scream or complain
to see a cockroach

instead she gave me
my own private recital
with some new numbers

that would mean you are
over a hundred years old
i quickly challenged

I'm sorry, his haikus are habit-forming. He replied

boss a cockroach life
has few events it lasts long
to provide content

Mortimer Mouse was broken-hearted to lose the inspiration for his uplifting volume <u>Keep Squeaking Through.</u>

Eventually he choked out his own version of her greatest number.

Cream cheese again
Camembert with a Dan-
Ish Samsoe and Emmental
And Monterey (Jack)
Keep Stilton blue
Add a Montagne Doux
With a bunch of triple cremes
And Wensleydale
Add some Fiore Sardo
With some old Manchego
And some fine Reblochon
And some Gran Padano
With an Asiago…

At this point his sobs turned into drooling, and he was unable to continue.

20 June

Whatever happened to Whatever Happened To stories? They regularly and reliably filled space in newspapers. I wrote quite a few myself in my hack days. It was always good for expenses to do a WHT? story, first because the former fameholder often took a long time to track and trace (of course we did not benefit then from the government's wonderful new system or systems as the case may be) and second because the former fameholder often required generous hospitality to entice him/her out of obscurity. (Eyes mist). Ah, those days when real newspapers pursued real stories requiring real expenses rather than recycling handouts and hashtags...

Prodnose: Don't you think hack nostalgia is a bit overdone?

Myself: Your expenses claims on the old Clarion were the only worthwhile fiction you ever produced.

He slunk in the direction of off. Sometimes he does rile me. Anyway, it's time to ask WHT Jo Moore, the apparatchik who once worked for the New Labour Cabinet minister Stephen Byers (himself a candidate for WHT and indeed WTF). Her name got onto the nation's lips for the email she sent out to her department's press office suggesting that 9/11 was "a very good day to get out anything we want to bury."

Jo Moore was of course a pioneer. It's now standard government practice to bury bad news on days of major events. Indeed, governments regularly manufacture bad news of their own to immolate stories which are far worse and far more important. Donald Trump does this all the time. He and his keepers are smart enough to manufacture stories which they can use twice or more (such as drinking bleach), first as the original story and then in responding to the furore.

Something majorly horrendous is about to happen to our country for which the government will be blamed. That is the only possible conclusion for the government's recent manufacture of not just one but two "bad" stories as a smokescreen.

The first was the painting of Boris Johnson's official aeroplane. This story is still doing an excellent job for the government in conventional and social media. Boris Johnson would be very foolish now to accept a decorator's estimate and have the thing actually painted. The more garish his plane, the smaller he will look when he steps out of it.

The second was manufactured by a forgotten minister from the political swamplands, Paymaster Penny Mordaunt, who called for two new Royal yachts to be built from overseas aid money. It was clever of her (or Dominic Cummings) to suggest two, which gave more "legs" to the story, encouraging arguments over the number as well as the principle of Royal yachts.

I must admit that in my giddy youth I coveted two identical floating gin palaces of my own, one to be called Gotit (subs, all one word) and the other Flauntit (subs ditto.) My fantasies are now much more tasteful. I shall wait for a 3 for 2 deal and commission three identical schooners to bob outside my island establishment in São Tomé e Príncipe. They will be called Luxe, Calme and Volupté.

21 June

The (London) Times reports that the Russians are grooming Saif Gaddafi to take power in Libya. This would certainly reflect their long-standing principle that no state under their influence should be governed better than Putin's Russia. That might give the Russian people or even Russian advisers the idea that they could do better for themselves than the kleptomaniac klutzes now running their country.

It gives me an excuse to repeat my poem (The Little Yellow Gadd) from years ago on the fall of Saif's father. I was pleased to have found a rhyme for Gaddafi.

There's a cross-eyed mad dictator by the shores of Tripoli
With the last remaining goons who take his pay,
Where new graves are dug for people who just wanted to be free,
And Tony Blair for ever looks away.

He was known as Mad Gaddafi by the sergeants in the Naafi[68]
Though he called himself a Colonel and a sage
But for all his planes and tanks, they despised him in the ranks,
As they lived through forty years of fear and rage.

In a desert tented throne he lived a life alone
With creatures to obey his every whim.
To the world outside he stank, for all his money in the bank –
Till Tony Blair arrived to smile at him.

Beneath the desert sun their hearts both beat as one.
They washed away their past with cups of tea.
As he whispered soothing lies the madman locked his eyes:
And Tony Blair saw what he chose to see.

He left serene and sunny, with gifts of oil and money,
And thought himself a statesman of renown.

---

[68] Acronym of the official organization which supplies retail and leisure services to Brtain's armed forces

But the people tossed a hammer at the tyrant
named Muammar
And they drove him out of every Libyan town.

And at last they made him hunker and cower in his
bunker,
The final shrivelled kingdom of the mad.
Taking calls from Tony Blair, as his people now
prepare
To take vengeance on their little yellow Gadd.

If Saif G is restored, I wonder if Blair and all his
other old mates will resume their acquaintance.
Perhaps Prince Andrew could pay him a state visit
as his first step in resuming Royal duties.

A Miss Aisha Gaddafi keeps emailing me to
promise a share of the family fortune if only she
could have all my bank details. Perhaps she'll stop
now, and get onto the earhole of her half-brother.

In Pakistan, the national cricket stadium in Lahore
is still known as the Gaddafi Stadium,

remembering the palmy days of friendship in the 1970s between Gaddafi M and Z A Bhutto. There have been long arguments over renaming it. Perhaps they will not bother now.

22 June

The Fake News media have reported that Donald Trump's live rally was a total frost, filled with empty seats, marked by a disjointed speech, and that he would have done better to stay 24 hours from Tulsa, as recommended by the great Gene Pitney. (I produced a London cover version "I was only 24 hours from Tulse Hill" but it failed to make the charts roar.)

With all the authority of someone who was not there, I can say that Trump walked (without a single stumble) over a substantial lake to attend the rally and addressed a crowd of several million worshippers. A collection of garments from the Presidential wardrobe was passed among them for them to kiss the hem of. After his speech, which was disjointed only by the "protracted and stormy applause" (© Pravda reporting Stalin) at each syllable, the President fed the entire crowd with a few loaves and fishes sent from the kitchens of the Trump Mar de Largo resort. Worshippers who asked for a vegetable were greeted by Vice-President Pence.

Prodnose: That joke comes from Thatcher's time.

Myself: Indeed, and now the roar passes to a new generation. In other news, Peter Mandelson (the one who isn't a malignant recurring virus) has again put himself forward to become head of the World Trade Organization. If he is really a serious contender, I may be forced to apply myself.

23 June

I have had to tell the neighbour that his cockatiel will never master chess. I hate to give up on any pupil (I taught the Dalai Lama everything he ever knew about cocktail mixes) but that bird never grasped the central point of the game. He thought it was all over as soon as he had managed to fianchetto his bishops. Getting the mighty mitres onto the long diagonals is an excellent manœuvre but it is not the be-all and end-all of the game, no more than going ding-ding-ding with the bell is the be-all and end-all of trolley car conducting.

He reminds me of a parrot I got to know in a pet shop during the first of my gap years. The pet shop owner was an affable cove, the father of two boy singers whom I sometimes accompanied on the piano. I wonder what happened to them? Anyway, petshop père simply could not offload this parrot. Guinea pigs were flying off his shelves as if they were guinea fowl…

Prodnose: Guinea fowl cannot fly…

Myself: Most species can, you cloth-headed correcter, until you get them in the oven with some garlic, olive oil, and a few strips of bacon, adding a dash of cooking sherry if you have not drained the staff in desperation after running out of very old Glen Maxwell Australian single-malt whisky ("makes a hit anywhere"). As I was saying, rabbits were leaping off his shelves as if they were hares.

His guppies disappeared as if they were puppies. But week after week the parrot remained in baleful reproach, devouring seed as if it were seed. As winter closed in, I decided to give my friend a helping hand. I dropped in regularly and taught the parrot to say in a pleading tone "Buy me, buy me for Christmas."

I was then called away for some months to advise Harold Wilson on the balance of payments. It was frightfully important in those days. The monthly trade figures, almost invariably dire, filled newspaper columns. BRITAIN IN THE RED AGAIN. Ministers would punch the cliché buttons to make solemn exhortations to the country: shoulders must be tightened and belts put to the wheel. Or something like that. Anyway, after long arguments with the Treasury Wilson adopted my simple suggestion of printing the monthly trade figures back to front. BOOMING BRITAIN IN THE BLACK. This, more than anything, secured his massive election victory in 1966. Whatever happened to the dear old balance of payments?

Anyway, when I returned to my friend's pet shop in the spring I was disappointed to find that my stratagem had failed. The wretched bird was still there, saying "Buy me, buy me for Christmas" proving only that he was well past what would later be called his sell-by date and inducing nervous fury in otherwise tranquil chinchillas.

I offered to teach it "My Way" instead but my friend reacted with a nervous fury of his own. "Haven't you done enough damage already?" he shrieked like a salamander and asked me to leave.

I later discovered that the bird had built a wonderful career in showbiz, but sadly only after death in the legendary Monty Python sketch.

24 June

"Xylophones hammered out a funky jazz quickstep to the crows in the waving baobabs." My eager public will recognize this as the opening sentence of my memoirs <u>My Goodness How I Roared!</u> Those who can remember as far back as April 30 will know the subsequent ones with the ylang-ylang and the zephyrs.

I have kept them waiting too long for what happened next. The hurly-burly of life at Rubato Towers has been too big a distraction. Moreover, my plan to monetize my memoirs has been a sad disappointment. There is a bear market in vanity. Or rather a mouse market. Only Mortimer offered me anything to be mentioned in a scene where a Famous Person met me. And that only to promote his own sugary uplifting work <u>Keep Squeaking Through </u>(for which I am providing most of the content in my sleep). And he offered only the inferior Brie from the cheese selection his publisher sent to him as an advance. And for this he expects to figure, with dialogue, mark you, in the scene with Nelson Mandela. Well, he got short shrift. The shortest shrift I have ever produced. No more than the sh in the iconic tonic water advertisements.

If that is his final offer, he will find himself written into Donald Trump's Cabinet. Meanwhile, I am withholding all of my dreams from him. Last night's zingers will show him what he is missing.

Some people can see the light at the end of the tunnel. Others put a tunnel in front of every light.

People who spend their lives in the middle of the road rarely get to the end of it.

Nobody knows the truffles I've seen. Apparently I sang that one. Mortimer originally transcribed it as "trifles." Which would have been silly.

With a general relaxation of lockdown, appropriately on Independence Day, thousands of cricket clubs were preparing for the return of competitive matches. They were scuppered at the last minute by our Dear Leader, who has just noticed that cricket makes use of a leather ball passed regularly through several different hands. Always eager to maintain a pretence of learning, he described this practice as a "vector" for Johnny Virus. In top-quality snooker matches, the ball regularly gets polished by a smartly dressed bird in white gloves. It's his one big moment in the proceedings. I am certain that some of these birds could be persuaded to appear in cricket matches. They would add tone to any ground.

I spent the rest of the day in high dudgeon. Mortimer, kafkaa and Rufus had to coax me down from the ceiling. kafkaa tried to improve my mood with a new anti-Trump haiku.

lets remove the dope
from the white house and get it
all back on the streets

25 June

In an attempt to justify his tardy and capricious decision to maintain the ban on recreational cricket, Boris Johnson suggested that its return might be the last straw that broke the back of a camel in a giant wheelbarrow. So cricket perishes in a charnel house of deranged metaphors…

Prodnose: Perhaps the Prime Minister was making one of those excursions into self-mocking irony which you often favour.

Myself: If it were deliberate rather than inept, it is inappropriate for a Prime Minister in a plague year. It is right for me as the boulevardier of world literature to entertain my discerning public in this way. But he should be talking to everybody. No one wants a Prime Minister who's perpetually winking to some secret audience as if to say "You and I know this is all a bit of fun." That's why Keir Starmer is having such success from following my advice to be a sobersides and restrain his natural gifts as an entertainer. He is a veritable Tommy Cooper in private. At my last soirée before lockdown he had the company roaring and that was before he had even started on my material. The Papal Nuncio whom I had let in to read the gas meter was rolling on my second-best Pakistan carpet and damaged one of the bibelots.

Johnson's effort has nothing on the mangled metaphors of Peter Mandelson (the man not the virus). I collected them in grim fascination when he ran Labour's election campaign of 2010. He praised Gordon Brown's granite-like resilience. (The one thing granite cannot do is to bounce back into shape. It either resists an impact or shatters.) He claimed that the Tories had underlined a key plank of Labour's programme. He suggested that Labour had put the country on the road to recovery but the Tories would pull the rug from under it. These efforts go a long way to explaining the Coalition government which we then had to endure.

I am worried that Mandelson might look like a strong candidate to head the World Trade Organization compared to the government's choice. Dr Liam Fox. As International Trade Secretary, he negotiated a post-Brexit trade deal with the Faeroes. But he failed to secure one with Rockall, Fair Isle, South East Iceland or either of the Utsires, North or South. Or indeed any of the other wonderful places you hear on radio waiting for the cricket commentary to resume.

Mandelson or Fox. Is this the best our country can offer for the World Trade Organization? If either got the job, he would convert new nations to mercantilism.

26 June

I am still in a stand-off with Mortimer Mouse, until he is ready to offer a reasonable price for a mention in my memoirs <u>My Goodness How I Roared!</u> However, I have thought of another ripping wheeze to monetize my life.

I shall offer it to localities where nothing seems to have happened. Of course some localities actually like it that way. I played cricket against a village which advertised itself proudly as "the place where Time goes to sleep." It was such a successful slogan that I cannot even remember the name of the village. But there are places which may be looking for a little more pizzazz, and for a reasonable price I am willing to make them sites where a Famous Person met me.

I have my hopes of Penge, which represents the South Pole for one of the buses which serves Rubato Towers. According to my London encyclopedia no one famous has been to Penge since around 1840 when William IV's widow, Queen Adelaide, dropped by to give them some almshouses. About forty years later they had a terrible murder, when Harriet Staunton was starved to death at a house in Penge, and I gather that they are still trying to live that down. So if Penge wants a historic Celebrity Visitor they have only to ask me, and meet the usual sliding scale of fees. It may be hard for anyone to imagine why Nelson Mandela went to Penge. But if the local worthies are willing to pay for him, Penge will become the place where he joined me for lunch.

The property market is having a bit of a revival and I might offer my services to estate agents. If they are finding a particular property hard to sell, they can pay me to list it in my memoirs as a place where I wrote one of my novels. (For a little extra I will give them a blue plaque.)

The beauty of this scheme is that it might very well be true. I have an address book from the 1970s that is filled only with my addresses. In one year I was forced to move very frequently, for the usual reason. Tough times at the turf. I tried to make up my losses at the dog track, but met the same problem in finding an animal which could overtake a traffic cone. One of my selections won the lead role in a remake of Lassie. She still hasn't come home.

27 June

I have just noticed that the United States, the UK and China are ruled respectively by a Trump, a twerp and a tramp…

Prodnose: Surely not? Whatever else you may say about Mr Xi he is always correctly groomed.

Myself: I have told you before to say Hsi. Had I been allowed, I would have continued … ler on human rights.

Prodnose: Trampler? There's no such word.

Myself: There is now. (I have called many words into being and revived even more. Trampler may now emerge from its dungeon in the Shorter

Oxford dictionary, blinking in the unexpected glare of currency. My favourite invention was grapefruityshod, which matches uncopyrightable as the longest word in the English language with no repeated letters. Sadly, there has been little need for a compact way to say "wearing footwear improvised from discarded grapefruit skins.")

My standoff continues with Mortimer Mouse. He will have no place in my memoirs and I maintain the embargo on my dreams. He passes me icily in Rubato Towers, insofar as a mouse can be icy although this is commonplace for a mousse or a moose.

I spent a long time staring at my hair in the mirror. A sad sight. My stylist removed most of it and shaped the rest just before lockdown. His efforts stood up remarkably well but now I would blush to meet my public. As I stared I heard a little voice: "I know thee not, old man, How ill white hairs become a fool and jester" followed by some characteristic squoars (and that's another of my inventions.)

I replied "If you are going to be Henry V you might check what he did to Mortimer", but my heart wasn't in it. The rodent was right. What am I but a perennial fool on the turf and a jester with an audience of one? The hairs say it all. They are a not a magnificent leonine mane as affected by flamboyant barristers. They are not a distinguished streak of grey, as affected by politicians seeking gravitas. (Long ago Harold Wilson was falsely accused of using a product called Silvilox for this purpose. He was also falsely accused of affecting his famous pipe in public and smoking cigars when he thought no one would find out. Not so. I can confirm that Wilson made life a misery for his intimates by puffing perpetually on a pipe filled with an especially mephitic shag which would have been banned on the battlefield.)

The majority of my hair now is neither magnificent or distinguished. It is simply white. Our Dear Leader has proclaimed July 6 as National Haircut Day. Another great British tradition will be restored as people camp all night (socially distanced one hopes) outside salons for the great reopening as they used to do for the start of the January sales.

Knowing this feckless government, I am certain they have made no special arrangements for disposal of the bushels of shorn hair on the great day. If conditions are windy they may swirl around our cities causing irritation and accidents. I certainly don't want any of Boris Johnson's in my face.

28 June

As if I have not enough creature discomforts on my hands, Rufus the Ruthless Ryukin has become unhinged by his recent triumphs in the bridgequarium. Recently he defeated an apparently castiron contract by Sheldon and Sheila the Smart Shubunkins in the only possible way by underleading the Ace-King-Queen-Jack-Ten of Spades to make an entry for his astonished partner Culbert the Comet, who then did the right thing by leading back a club. (Dismiss, readers, the unworthy thought that the hand was dealt as a goulash, for such deals are banned under the stern playing conditions of the bridgequarium.)

Rufus now asks me to get the hand, with his commentary, published in <u>Garden Bridge</u>, the popular recreational journal which tried to sue Boris Johnson for using their name for his silly vanity project during his time as London Mayor. Worse still, he wants me to promote his new convention: over any pre-emptive bid an immediate Four Clubs asks partner to bid whichever major he or she does not have. Of course he intends to name this convention Modern Fishbein.

"Rufus, I hate to be a piker… piker… [Sighs] Never mind, but I fear that your new gadget may be too difficult to remember for social bridge players and could generate recriminations and even divorces." (I remembered Judge Cocklecarrot in the old days scattering decrees nisi like confetti to petitioners who presented evidence of spousal bidding errors.)

"Richard," he replied loftily insofar as a goldfish can be lofty, "My work, like yours, is directed at the expert not hoi polloi."

I was so impressed that he remembered that it is otiose to say "the hoi polloi" as so many do, since "hoi" means "the", that I was unable to remonstrate instantly…

Prodnose: This will have to stop. No one will believe that you can talk to a goldfish.

Myself (removing a stray heart-shaped fish flake from lapels of evening wetsuit): During my stay in Xcalak (see 23 April) I was taught the art of fish-whispering by the local Ouishi Ouashi tribe, who as even you should know are keepers of the sacred Mayan lake of Ouatsupdoc and believe me, the fish make such a racket in that lake you can't even hear the foxes at night.

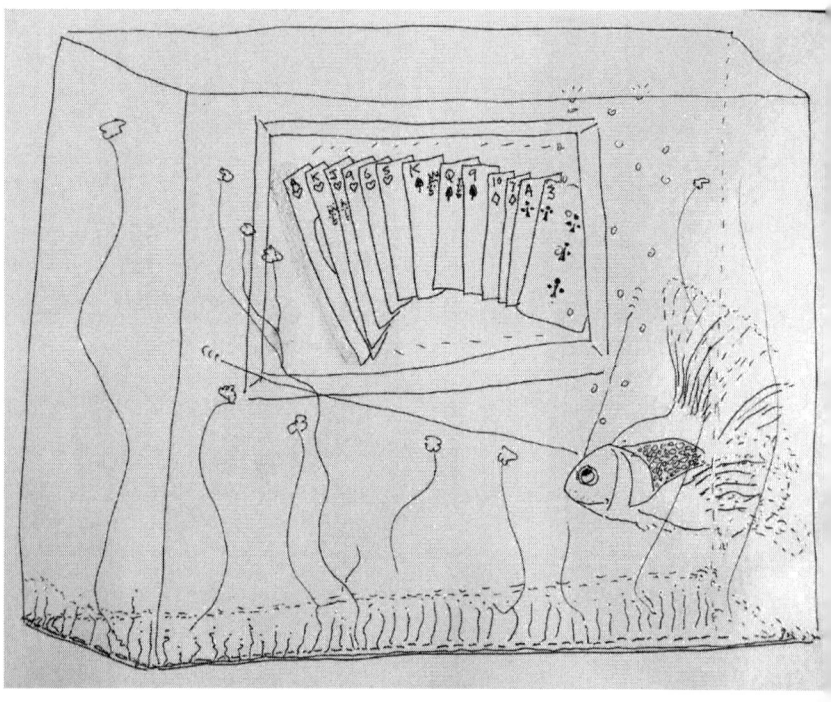

Rufus the Ryukin, now master of the bridgequarium

29 June

There was an uncommon visitor in the car park garden of Rubato Towers, assessing the luxury motors on which the foxes used to recline after fornication. (They have been welcome absentees in recent days and I trust that they have found a better location for their intended all-screeching all-dancing porno video.)

"Why, Mr Toad!" I exclaimed. "Forgive me, but I thought you were serving an eighteen-year sentence for cheeking the police. What are you doing amongst us in Rubato Towers? Policing the chic?" My goodness, how I roared, but predictably alone. My visitor fixed me with a … a… (punches cliché button) … a baleful stare.

"I think…" (I'm so sorry: I have not done justice to his faintly Continental accent. Punches cliché button again.) "I zink you mistake me for annuzer. My name is Jacques Bavarder."

My French is a trifle rusty. It has been a long time since my last visit to the great jazz festival in the chateau of the amorous Comte Baiser, for whom I am a regular closing act on the piano. It took me a few moments to give out the expected "You mean?…"

"Exacte. I am a natterjack toad."

"We are indeed honoured. Can I offer you a few woodlice?"

"Non, merci. But are you able to recommend a good local garage?" He gestured towards a scaled-down Lagonda in the car park. It had clearly once been elegant and a faultless freesia still fluttered in its plant holder. But it had been badly dented by its impact with the garbage container (normally a popular restaurant with the foxes) and the double overhead magneto cranking shaft was protruding at a most peculiar angle. I have become quite a shrewd judge of these matters. So it was true after all. Toads are terrible drivers.

I asked my visitor his business in Rubato Towers. He became very furtive. His bulging eyes darted around the empty car park. I offered him assurance.

"We can't be heard in here."

"Pardon?"

"I said we can't be heard in here."

"Pardon?" I was gratified to see a French amphibian so au fait with the routines of British pantomime. He then explained his astonishing secret mission.

He has formed a social enterprise business called Creature Restraint in association with representatives of other endangered wildlife species. They offer environmental campaigners a means to bring any noxious development to a grinding halt. One of their number will simply appear at the site to be recorded and filmed. The developer then has to clear dozens of new hurdles before he or she can do any further works, including the creation of a new perfect habitat for the endangered creature. Many ghastly projects are then abandoned in despair. Depending on the site in question, Creature Restraint can also supply a great crested newt, a barn owl, any number of bats, an otter, or an adder. For the discount market (minor supermarket extensions) they currently have a three-for-two offer on common dormice.

The scientific name for natterjack toad is *Epidalea calamita* (clearly bestowed by a frustrated developer). They are still thriving in France but my new friend cleverly spotted the business opportunity for him and his companions in the denuded British Isles. He was on his way to a worthy neighbour, to help him prevent another example of the monstrous carbuncles which blight the view from Rubato Towers. I escorted him to his client, wishing him the atheist version of Godspeed. I offered him a few elocution lessons. In this febrile pre-Brexit period it might be dangerous for a French toad to block a patriot developer such as Richard Desmond[69]: FROG FRAUD WRECKS JOB HOPES.

Well, I never. Had I but known of this business I might have stopped the Shard. The Gherkin. The Cheesegrater.[70] The Tongue Depressor. (I made that one up.) I will not give any further details since I am not totally certain as to its legality. But if

---

[69] Property developer, former media owner, recently accused of bribing a Cabinet minister to approve one of his developments.
[70] Garish high-rise buildings in London.

anyone out there needs the services of a questing vole, I know where to find one.

30 June

A long Zoom call with Keir Starmer. He is finding it agonizing to follow my advice to present himself as Mr Sobersides. He yearns to show voters his true self as Cheeky Keir, the Bad Boy of the Halls. He performed a set of his best "turns", for all the world as if auditioning for a spot on the pier at Blackpool in its great days.

I feel his pain. The turns are hog-whimperingly funny, not that I have ever heard a hog whimper, but dear old "Piggy" Emsworth assures me that they do in moments of exaltation. Keir's performance had an electrifying impact on my household.

The card-crazed goldfish quartet passed out 84 consecutive deals in the bridgequarium.

kafkaa the cockroach had all 10,000 lenses glued to the screen and then composed three instant verselets for the performer.

keep calmer
vote for starmer

good karma
vote for starmer

the answers clear
vote for keir

Mortimer Mouse was totally stagestruck. He abandoned his long stand-off with me and offered me all the cheese in the world to write him into the scene in my memoirs where Keir first met me.

But I had to pronounce the traditional stern words to the auditioner: "Leave your name. But not with us."

He was crestfallen, so I continued more gently in the idiom of Simon Cowell. "Keir, you smashed it! But your party and your country need you to hide your talent. Boris Johnson is the David Brent of British politics. He is idle, he is incompetent, he is way over-promoted but he still expects to be loved as an entertainer. Voters are sick of his schtick. They don't want another Prime Minister like that. They want solid competence from a boring details kind of guy. If you want a simple slogan to run against him: But Seriously…"

I was on a roll. "Stop being matey-blokey plain Keir. Remind people that you were a distinguished public servant. Use your full title, the Right Honourable Sir Keir Starmer Queen's Counsel Knight Commander of the Order of the Bath. I like the sound of Commander. If you need a short version, be Commander Starmer. You could rename the Labour party the Bath party, oh no, wait, that didn't work too well in Iraq…"

His crest was still fallen. In fact, he looked utterly woebegone, although that's always been a damn silly word since if you are woebegone your woe clearly isn't begone. He looked utterly woedrenched. I continued still more gently.

"Save those wonderful turns for Downing Street, where they will enrapture state visitors. The EU will beg us back in on any terms. Donald Trump will become a good President. However, I think you will have to drop the turn in the garter belt. I am sure it wowed them at the Prosecutors Smoker years ago, but in these times too many people will find it 'transgressive'". He of course detected without irritating finger gestures my attitude to this fashionable buzzword.

"Remain Mr Serious. When you need to pep yourself up in the polls, you can always sack a Shadow Minister. You've got far too many of them already and I can give you a little list that would none of them be missed. Look at A, B and C…"

The leader cut in instantly. "Why do you think I appointed them?"

He will go far.

1 July

I have booked a hair appointment with my long-established artist. I imagine my terrible hair cascading to the floor. It will take a great weight off my mind, literally. MGHIR! The one snag is that I left it too late to get the appointment on National Hair Day next Monday, and must have it the day after. So as thousands of others proudly parade their new heads, I will be forced to slink into the salon under a trilby, hoping that none of my public will recognize me. Strangers' fingers may point as to the figure in the H M Bateman cartoon: The Man Who Left It Too Late To Phone The Salon.[71] I may have to revive one of the outfits I used during bad times on the turf.

An especially doltish performance by Boris Johnson presenting his misnamed New Deal inspires an

---

[71] A famous series of men making embarrassing social faux pas by British cartoonist H M Bateman.

especially magisterial riposte from my friend Marina Hyde.

https://www.theguardian.com/commentisfree/2020/jun/30/conservatives-cowboy-builders-boris-johnson

I ask her whether she can bear to waste such prose on him, and put to her my recent reflections on Jonathan Swift (see 28 May.) Within Marina's piece I discover a magisterial review of Johnson's book on Churchill. It begins with the ridiculously flattering statement that Johnson's prose feels like a long harangue for hours by Bertie Wooster. If only… The review revealed Johnson's assertion that the Germans captured Stalingrad during the Second World War. That says a lot to me. We are being governed by someone who does not know a basic fact or does not care about it, who employs an army of helpers of the same kind.

Although apparently very late for its publisher, Johnson's Churchill book was evidently knocked off in a hurry. He is the supreme knocker-off.

Before becoming a minister he earned ... (punches cliché button) ... eye-watering sums of money for knocking off articles, speeches, books. He became the Pericles of piffle.

Prodnose: You're jealous.

Myself: Of course I am jealous, but many a jealous witness has given truthful evidence in the box. (Flicks imaginary gown in manner of Boyd QC making a telling point.) In my own days as a full-time hack, I frequently knocked off pieces in a hurry for my old newspaper, often on important topics such as the future of legspin bowling. Some of these gave me such shame that I asked for them to be published under the name of Phil Space (now berthed in <u>Private Eye</u>) or Will Thisdo. I hope I have atoned since by a daily effort to raise English prose to heights never before attempted, let alone achieved.

I too was a very good knocker-off but I did not expect to govern the country as a result. Boris Johnson has never really left his old trade. He knocks off a New Deal. He knocks off Brexit. He knocks off the virus. Unfortunately, all this stuff is important.

2 July

"The new normal" is a sappy trope which has me reaching for my revolver. For that matter, so is trope.

But the "new normal" has an underlying truth. What is normal and familiar has tremendous power over people's lives.

Thousands of batters are dismissed in cricket in the same way year after year, week after week, attempting a stroke that is normal but fatal (in my case the elegant last-minute whip off the pads which effortlessly diverts the leather traveller towards the perimeter at fine leg.) There may be temporary remorse and abstinence, but more likely the perpetrator will say proudly "That's the way I play". In either case, the stroke will be attempted again, and again, with the same result. LBW even from the most sympathetic or bribed umpire.

Thousands of people return regularly to restaurants or pubs (when open) which they do not like, and order dishes and beverages there which they do not like, because they are familiar.

My old friend John Mortimer had a divorce practice. In saying farewell to successful clients he would often murmur "See you again in five years." He was right of course. People form relationships over and over again which do not work, and may even be abusive, because they are familiar. Such relationships may well make people assume that they are worthless, but that is less terrifying to them than the unknown.

I am starting to think that the Tories are trying to make bad government "the new normal." The master plan is to govern so badly for long enough as to make the British people habituated to it. If they succeed the British people will assume that nothing better is possible. (Pollsters might like to ask voters the last good government they remember and work out the median age of those who can name one.) With a daily dripfeed of scandals, blunders and lies the British people will cease to react to the next scandal, blunder or lie. By then they will believe that they deserve nothing better than their expensively educated clot of a Prime Minister, his absurdly inflated adviser, his ministers who are barely worth bribing, the cowed civil servants saying "Yes minister," and meaning it. When that happens the Tories will call a snap election.

They may not have time to bring the British people to that point. It is just possible that Keir Starmer (Commander Starmer if he takes my advice) may offer them the prospect of honest, diligent government.

In that case the Tories will fall back on Plan B. They will dump Boris Johnson and replace him with an alternative leader who can give voters a better impression of empathy and competence. A trained gerbil could achieve this. They will then fight a "give him/her a chance" election.

I believe that Donald Trump was pursuing the same strategy of making outrageously bad government the new normal. But it has not worked. The American people are far less submissive than the British. They complain about poor service, whether from seaside hotels (see 11 May) or national government. Rather than go down with Trump, the Republican party may be about to fall back on Plan B. For constitutional reasons they are unable to replace Trump with a gerbil, and they will have to make the best of Mike Pence.

Prodnose: Haven't you made enough jokes about Mike Pence?

Myself: No. (Half to myself) Bumbling bloviating booby who gives mediocrity a bad name.

Mortimer Mouse, kafkaa, Rufus Ryukin: To whom do you refer? (I have trained them well.)

Myself: To whomever you please.

<u>3 July</u>

Mortimer Mouse had a meltdown. I found him in a puddle of tears. I remembered his response to the passing of Dame Vera Lynn, but could think of none other which might have inspired a similar cascade. Had I never known in all these years that he was a cricket-lover, grieving for the last of the great West Indian three Ws, Sir Everton Weekes?

"It was the first great innings I ever saw," I told the blubbering rodent. "His 90 in a lost cause for the West Indies at Lords in 1957, 16 fours, and my first glimpse of the future genius of Gary Sobers who made 66…" Amazingly, this narrative failed to grip.

But then I realized the cause of his melancholy. He had found a book I had preserved and cherished from my childhood: <u>Walter The Lazy Mouse</u> by the noted Marjorie Flack. My heartstrings were not just tugged but twanged. I eased the book away from him before he could shed further tears. It was a potentially valuable first edition from 1937 with Marjorie's original drawings and a few lucid notes from my six-year-old self. He was seriously threatening its re-sale value.

I should have kept it safe from him. Avid members of my public will recall that Mortimer first appeared in my front room in Rubato Towers, selling The Big Issue. At that time, my suite was far from soignée. Only a homeless mouse would want to live there. And who was the central character of Marjorie's story? A homeless mouse.

Walter lives in a large mouse family, but he is so lazy that he can never keep up with family events. His repeated absences make his family forget about him entirely. When they move home, he is left behind. He returns home from school (late as usual) and finds it totally empty and with no forwarding address. He rushes desperately through Mouse Village trying to find his family, without success. He leaves the Village altogether and finds himself in a dark wood, hungry and friendless. He collapses in tears. This is the point where I found Mortimer.

Things get a little better for Walter: he forms a new surrogate family with three frogs and a turtle. He builds a new home and a new school. He meets his old family again and they give him a new set of clothes – but he ends up with his surrogate family.

As with so much classic children's literature, one can only imagine the rejection letters that this work would have collected today. Most publishers would have told Marjorie that it would give young children acute separation anxiety. A few might a have invited her to rewrite it for "an older demographic" with gritty realism. Mouse Village would have become a nightmarish Mouse City where Walter descends into a dark drug world of mousecaline and skunk.

Marjorie and her feckless publishers (Doubleday) never imagined the impact of her actual plot on a real mouse.

"That's me," he ... he... (punches cliché button) ... choked out between sobs.

Prodnose: Come, you can do better than that.

Myself: Still not quite myself. (Takes deep draught of Fernet-Branca mixture and punches cliché button harder.) Racking sobs.

"I was abandoned by my family too. But Walter at least found his again. I never did. And they never looked for me. I'm the mouse nobody wants. Not even mice." He sobbed even harder. It was time for one of Plato's Noble Lies.

"I want you, Mortimer."

I was proud of my performance. It was a match for Rex Harrison talking his way through "I've Grown Accustomed To Her Face."

"You're part of my world at Rubato Towers. I cannot reveal you to the neighbours. Sadly, we have some murophobes in our midst. And some katsaridaphobes, so kafkaa too must be kept secret. But all the Famous People who know me. They always ask after you. The Obamas. Both of them on their last Zoom call. Could not get them down to business at all. 'How's that Mortimer?' and I had to give them all your latest cheesy sayings for the next hour. Glad the call was on their nickel."

His sobs diminished slightly.

"The same with Ben Stokes. Called to get my tactical advice for the first lockdown Test against the West Indies. But first it was 'how's your mousy mate, not caught in the leg trap I hope?'"

That was a bit of a floater. "I might as well throw myself on a trap. You needn't bother with any cheese," and his pity party resumed.

"That's just 'banter', Mortimer. It's part of cricket today. And as for the Queen... I had to turn her down again when she asked about forming a government of national salvation. Straight away she snapped, 'Not you, I meant Mortimer.'"

No impact. I pushed on.

"I want you here, Mortimer." I channelled Rex Harrison. "Your smiles, your frowns, your ups, your downs are second nature to me now. I need your book to work on, <u>Keep Squeaking Through,</u> almost as much as I need my own memoirs. Without you, whom would I dream for?" It gave me a sudden inspiration. I hurtled to the piano.

(Sings) For whom would I dream,
Or take one for the team
Or work up some steam
Unless it were you?
Unless it were you... (plunk-plunketty-plunk)

I knew it would be hard to find a performer who cared enough about grammar to use "whom" and the subjunctive, but lyrics should not be an excuse for laxity.

I accompanied this with the soupiest chords I could think of. None of my beloved major sevenths. I banished George Gershwin and Jerome Kern and summoned up Irving Berlin at his soupiest.

As often happens with my piano playing, it made listeners forget what they were doing (in his case being convulsed with sobs) and look up. "I'm channelling Irving Berlin, Mortimer," I told him as I continued to vamp. "Although one of the most successful songwriters of all time, he could play the piano in only one key, E flat…"

Prodnose: That's one more than you.

I ignored his crass interruption. I still had a disconsolate mouse on my hands. I continued "For whom would I care… Over to you." I vamped and vamped. Slowly my companion's little mouth began to turn upwards, although it required a trained eye to detect this. Eventually he opened it and squeaked out "For whom would I dare…" I vamped on and he worked his little mouth. Then he squeaked "Fight a tiger or bear" and we both sang "Unless it were you" twice to plunk-plunketty-plunk.

"Over to you for the bridge," I told him over some alternative vamping.

After a while he came up with "You are the cheese on my toastie You are the cheese on my cheese…" Not what I would have chosen for commercial success, but I was glad to see him looking a lot more consolate.

"Er, bridges are always a problem. Ask Boris Johnson. Look here's kafkaa," pointing out the roach, who had come up to enjoy the performance. "He claims to be a professional poet, ask him to help you." I explained matters to the roach and skipped out for my laptop. I then vamped a little more. Before long the roach headbutted on the machine

youre my special mail from the postie

Mortimer rushed over to confer with him, and eventually squeaked out "You make my whole life a breeze." By now he was fully consolate and totally engaged on completing a soupy song to go into his uplifting volume <u>Keep Squeaking Through.</u> I vamped verse and bridge a few more times, recorded them, switched on the machine and tiptoed away as rodent and roach worked on fresh words.

When I returned half an hour later they were bawling and yelling at each other like Gilbert and

Sullivan when the former tried to rhyme Iolanthe with fancy. As they say up in Northern parts, there were words spoken, and language used. But I knew that I had completed the redemption of Mortimer Mouse. I slipped away to my dinner party in a celebratory mood, as subsequent events confirmed.

<u>4 July</u>

By popular demand

Unless It Were You   Lyrics by Mortimer Mouse and kafkaa roach   Vague vamping by Ricky Rubato

For whom would I dream   *Eb*
Or take one for the team   *Cm7*
Or work up some steam   *Cm7*
Unless it were you?   *Fm7 sus*
Unless it were you   *Fm7*

For whom would I care
For whom would I dare
Fight a tiger or bear

Unless it were you?
Unless it were you

You are the cheese on my toastie *Fm7*
You are the cheese on my cheese *Bb6*
You're my special mail from the postie *F7 Bb*
You make my whole life a breeze.   *F7 Bb*

For whom would I pine
And hope for a sign
That one day you'd be mine
Unless it were you?
Unless it were you

For whom would I long
With a love that's so strong
As to beg for in song
Unless it were you?
Unless it were you.

You are the beats in my haiku
Five seven five all in threes:
I'm trying to say that I like you
Even more than my cheese.

For whom would I mope
And act like a dope
And try to soft soap
Unless it were you?
Unless it were you.

For whom would I dream
And constantly scheme
And wait for love's gleam
Unless it were you?
Unless it were you. *Final Eb*

Independence Day. I shared it years ago with the Duke and Duchess of Windsor at Cash Mountain, the Giltfrees' estate overlooking the Black Hills of Dakota. (The estate was broken up and sold as building lots when George Giltfree, against my advice, tried to corner the US whitebait market.) I always remember what dear Wallis wrote in the visitors book: "Here on the Fourth with my third."

Years ago an enterprising reporter typed up the Declaration of Independence without identifying it and asked fifty people to sign it on the streets of Miami. Only one accepted the invitation. Several thought the Declaration was "commie stuff", one threatened to call the police, another the FBI. In a separate exercise, the majority of a group of 300 high school students failed to recognize it, and over a quarter of them thought it had been written by Lenin.

This year I arranged for the Declaration to be put to the eleven surviving people who have been elected President or Vice-President of the United States. (Jimmy Carter, 96, and Walter Mondale, 91, are the oldest pair of survivors in American history.) Nine spotted it at once. One was a Don't Know. One recognized it but claimed to have written it himself.

5 July

Living with Mortimer Mouse after his redemption is like living with Bingo Little after Jeeves has extracted him from the soup.

Prodnose: Surely you mean Bertie Wooster?

Myself: If you were familiar with the Master's œuvre, you would know that Bertie's gratitude is restrained, often confined to resigned acceptance of the destruction of his favourite garments under Jeeves's iron. It is Bingo who disturbs the Drones with incesant (Drones spelling) singing. And so it is with Mortimer, with that infernal ditty "Unless It Were You" which kafkaa and I helped him compose. Mortimer's range is limited as a vocalist and he has trouble with even the limited chord palette I assigned to him. He squeaks as much as sings. In fact he squings. He was delighted with my new term and is planning a debut collection called Squing Time.

In this ebullient mood Mortimer has no need of my dreams to fill his slushy volume Keep Squeaking Through. His latest efforts are all his own work.

Life's sunspots are not really spots. They're parts of the Sun that are just a bit cooler than the rest.

If at first you don't succeed, try, try, and try again. If then you don't succeed, redefine success.

When life bowls you searing yorkers, keep glancing them to leg. (I think that was under my influence even if I did not dream it.)

Mortimer's mood is bearable only because I am pretty bucked myself. Recreational cricket is to be restored after all next weekend. The agent for this was Mr Nick Ferrari. <u>Wisden</u> should honour him in next year's edition. On LBC radio Mr Ferrari induced Boris Johnson to say on air something so cringemakingly stupid about cricket as to embarrass even himself and compel a screaming U-turn within hours.

I wonder if Mr Ferrari could be induced to perform this service each day. It might offer the country some hope of competent administration. Since I shall now be busy with cricket after all, I have suggested Mr Ferrari to the Queen as head of her government of national salvation.

6 July

Good news keeps rolling in. Mr Jared Kushner has taken charge of the plummeting re-election campaign of his father-in-law Donald Trump. I am now vastly more confident of the success of my old friend Joe Biden.

The Journal of Molluscan Studies has produced another groundbreaking article, this time on "Use of tree resin as a food source by Galápagos snails." As if this topic were not gripping enough, the article offers "a novel hypothesis for the fossilization of snails in amber."

Nadia the tiger lives! I had supposed her a victim of the virus, being personated in the Bronx Zoo to spare Donald Trump from popular outrage. But no, it's the real Nadia. She finally came through with the answer to my special question. No impostrix, however well-prepared, could remember the details of the time when I took a thorn from her paw.

Rufus the Ruthless Ryukin continues to triumph in the bridgeaquarium. He and his now junior partner Culbert the Comet have been invited, as Team Rufus, to compete in the world's first virtual subaqua bridge tournament (originally to have been held at the new French resort of Les-Trois-Trèfles sur mer".)

Mortimer Mouse has been asked to endorse one of Britain's leading mail-order cheese companies ("The Cheddar's in the post"). And they've made him a non-executive director.

"You mean?..." I asked obligingly.

"Yes," he squeaked, "I'm going to sit on the cheese board." I did my best to roar for him.

British publishing is very old-fashioned and one of the most dread sights for any author is the sign of his or her self-addressed envelope with thick contents. I saw another such in reception at Rubato Towers. But for once it was not one of mine. The pernickety hand on the envelope was that of Reginald Prodnose. Without even holding the envelope up to the light I could tell it represented rejection by some thoughtful publishing house (I may buy some of their shares) of his collected criticism, rashly titled <u>The Last Word.</u> I watched the trembling author open the envelope. He glimpsed briefly at the covering letter. It must have been a particularly sulphurous rejection. He did not even expostulate or curse as we authors usually do. I have seen a few ashen people and mice in my time, but he was by some way the ashenest.

Poor Prodnose! He will always have a place in my salons when they resume. He gives my guests unsurpassed opportunities for a put-down. He is the conversational equivalent of the long-hop bowled in old cricket matches in India when His Highness the Maharajah came in to bat. "Would it please your Highness to hit this?" and off would speed the leather traveller through the admiring fielders, not so much intercepted as escorted to the boundary.

The only thing which could cheer me more than bad news for Prodnose is the same for Peter Mandelson (the man not the virus.)

And he's having plenty. His old chum Ghislaine Maxwell arrested and jailed, with no good option except to tell stories to the prosecutors of all the people she introduced to Jeffrey Epstein. (To encourage her, they might well transfer her to Sing-Sing prison with all the other "canaries.")

And now a story accusing him of truckling to China's totalitarian dictatorship at the behest of a sinister secret society set up years ago by the Chinese Communist party. This is most unfair. Mandelson is perfectly capable of truckling to totalitarian dictators at his own behest.

At this stage the "optics" of both stories are very bad for him. He has about as much chance of becoming the next Director General of the World Trade Organization as I have of winning the Derby on a rocking horse (although that would have progressed faster than the horses I have actually backed for the event.)

Poor Peter! How simply frightful! How humiliating! How delightful! Does he now regret not telling Ghislaine in the Eighties that he was too busy washing his hair? When China's Mr Hsi invited him to a tea party in 2018, would that he had said "Alas, your Paramountcy I am trapped at home waiting for a plumber…"

A Reader's Voice: Is there no good news for poor kafkaa?

Myself: In the present climate, it can be only a matter of time.

<u>7 July</u>

As I expected, kafkaa got his burst of good news. But it began with a confession and an amazing revelation.

boss i guess ya know
i aint your old pal archy
hes my smart cousin

I recognized my cue again. Looking as flabbergasted as I could manage, I babbled "You mean…?"

i know that dont mean
much because we roaches have
giant families

but archys real smart
he can write long epic verse
not just paltry hai
oh shit
kus

And his 10,000 lenses began to well up with tears. By now I was quite experienced in dealing with blubbering creatures and I waited for him to finish, while ensuring that he did not damage any potentially valuable book or bibelot. It was time for more Noble Lies. I rounded up the usual suspects, all the Famous People who know me and ask about him every time, and then said "Who says you can't write longer verse, too, kafkaa? You knocked off the best lines in Mortimer's soppy song Unless It Were You." My pep talk seemed to work. I could

see the little chap stiffening such sinews as he had.
At any minute he would summon up the blood.

"There's nothing to writing longer verse, kafkaa.
Just do some prose, when you think you've done
enough go to the next line and hey presto, it's
verse. Try it. Stay in lower case, it suits you, and
you can't copyright a case."

archy and me was always close

"Eight whole syllables! Was that hard?" He
continued in a trance.

he taught me everything i know
even that stuff only he could have known
from his visit here
he liked it here boss
he thought i might like it too

"If he liked it so much, why did he leave so suddenly?" kafkaa then made his amazing revelation. archy had fancied a look at the London Library. He slipped himself one day into a bag of books I was returning (the ones I kindly borrowed from unborrowed authors, see 3 April) and slipped out before I reached the Returns Desk. He liked the place so much that he decided to live there. He made himself a nice berth behind the pipes in the ancient gentleman's lavatory above the Reading Room. But then he heard of an appeal to rebuild it, so he took up a new residence behind the Fiction H shelves which house my novels.

Well, he won't be disturbed there.

when i lost my last place
i stayed with him for a bit
but archy thought the library wouldnt suit me
so he sent me here boss
i hope ya dont think that
a liberty

"No, but…. How did you get here? Did you both wait for me to come back with a book bag?"

of course not

I could hear him suppress the word "doofus."

he told me to take the 453 bus
like anyone else
listen ya really think
i could write a verse epic

"Of course." A strange light danced in his eyes, ten thousand times over.

i gotta see
da mouse

(Later) kafkaa announced his good news. It will deliver him from the long shadow of his smart cousin. He will become a poet in his own right. He had a long talk with Little Brown, publishers of Mortimer's forthcoming volume Keep Squeaking Through. He persuaded them that his cheesy sentiments would sound even more uplifting if accompanied by his backstory as a homeless mouse. He secured a handsome advance. And now archy's life of mehitabel will have a worthy successor: kafkaa's life of mortimer.

Today is the Seventh of the Seventh. I don't normally go in for number mumbo jumbo but when I take stock it does look like a magic day.

Nadia the tiger is alive and well.

The Journal of Molluscan Studies, overcoming any problems from the virus, continues to advance the frontiers of knowledge about our invertebrate chums.

The fornicating foxes have found a better location than Rubato Towers for their porn video.

Prodnose has been abashed (I glimpsed at the rejection letter he received. My goodness, how I roared! But it would be too cruel to share it.)

I have launched a goldfish into the world of bridge, and a mouse and a cockroach into the world of literature.

donald trump
in such a slump
he may jump
to beat the dump

(An excursion into rap by kafkaa).

Recreational cricket restored to England. Boris Johnson exposed by the issue as such an egregious ass that his authority will never recover. The resurgent Labour party in the stern grip of my client, Commander Starmer.

Mandelson the virus at bay. Mandelson the politician heading for history's brimming dustbin.

And for myself? Heading later for my first post-lockdown haircut. At last able to meet my public, the first of them in the cricket nets. What a difference it will make to the zombie, the zamboni, the zooter, the zorker (continues Volume 948) to bowl them with a proper coiffure.

This represents a set of multiple happy endings. That always worked best for Charles Dickens, so I think it the right time to close this diary. I intend to publish it, with a few extra pensées and songs, in the near future under the title The Prisoner Of Rubato Towers. Until then, farewell my beloved followers. I may post some more epithets against selected persons as they occur to me, or some progress reports from Mortimer, kafkaa and Rufus.

Coming soon: Lockdown Craziness: The Second Wave.

8 July

A Mouse Writes: It would be hard cheese of me not to thank all the wonderful people who have been following me through Richard's diary. You all have a very special place in my mousy heart. If I have reached out to just one person with the happy thoughts in my forthcoming collection Keep Squeaking Through, once again, slowly, Keep …Squeaking …. Through, to be published by Little Brown it makes my whole life worthwhile. And to anyone out there having a hard time, remember: life is just the bread in your sandwich of dreams.

a roach writes;

that goes for me too
i mean thanks to all those folks

following me
and thanks to richard
for introducing me to mortimer mouse
hes my inspiration
all those tough times
and he keeps squeaking through
as you folks will see
from my forthcoming life of mortimer
to be published by little brown
and thanks to richard for teaching me the trick of
free verse
its a breeze
when you know how

A Goldfish Writes: Six Spades, all pass. Sorry, things were a bit intense in the bridgequarium. Thank you to Richard for taking me in hand – the hand in question being one of bridge. MGHIR! Thank you to all the enthusiasts I have met through him. I will try from time to time to answer correspondents. My first being Esther from Sydenham. Esther, the disaster was entirely your partner's fault. In the sequence you gave me, your Four No-Trumps was clearly not a slam invitation but an SOS to say "I cannot stand your suit, I expect you to have at least nine of it." Don't take back his Diamond ring without a major apology. In Hearts.

A Pedant Writes: I am preparing an annotated version for publication of Richard Heller's diary, pointing out the many errors, particularly those related to myself. RIP. (Reginald Ixworth Prodnose.)

Richard Heller is a Master of the Arts of Oxford University and of many other arts besides. He went to Repton School and Balliol College. He was a long-serving humorous columnist on *The Mail On Sunday* and more briefly on *The Times*. He was also the main non-fiction book reviewer for *The Mail On Sunday* for seven years. He worked in the movie business in the United States and the UK, including a brief engagement on a motion picture called *Cycle Sluts Versus The Zombie Ghouls*. He wrote two cricket-themed novels *A Tale Of Ten Wickets* and *The Network*. He appeared in two finals on BBC Television's *Mastermind:* one of his specialist subjects was Sir Garry Sobers. He was chief of staff to Denis Healey, then Deputy Leader of the Labour Party, and Gerald Kaufman, then Shadow Home Secretary. With Peter Oborne he wrote *White On Green*, celebrating the drama of Pakistan cricket, shortlisted for the MCC/Cricket Society book of the year in 2017. They are currently making podcasts to relieve the cricket-deprived.

https://chiswickcalendar.co.uk/blogs-podcasts/#cricket-podcast

The author ready for his public after the post lockdown haircut by Robert at Atherton Cox.

Rupert Macnee is a creator and producer of television series in England, Canada and the United States, including profiles of Marvel's Stan Lee, comic artist Jim Steranko, and the creators of Dudley Doright. He studied drawing at the Otis Parsons School in Los Angeles, and developed the character of John Kniteright, a legendary English tabloid journalist. Rupert's father was the actor Patrick Macnee, who portrayed the immaculate secret agent John Steed in *The Avengers*.